# the stitch clique

## Sophia's Struggle

# the stitch clique

## Sophia's Struggle

**by tina wells**

**illustrations by mike segawa**

WEST MARGIN PRESS

*For my nephews Alexander and Maxwell*

© 2023 by Tina Wells

Illustrations by Mike Segawa

All rights reserved. No part of this book may be reproduced or transmitted in any form or by any means, electronic or mechanical, including photocopying, recording, or by any information storage and retrieval system, without written permission of the publisher.

ISBN: 9781513135076

Printed in the USA
27 26 25 24 23  1 2 3 4 5

Published by West Margin Press®

WestMarginPress.com

Proudly distributed by Ingram Publisher Services

WEST MARGIN PRESS
Publishing Director: Jennifer Newens
Marketing Manager: Alice Wertheimer
Project Specialist: Micaela Clark
Editor: Olivia Ngai
Design & Production: Rachel Lopez Metzger

# one

*Sophia Ito looks around her room once more, triple-checking to make sure she didn't miss anything. Retainer? Check. Toothbrush? Check. Toiletries? Check. Undies? Check. Amazing outfits that will trick everyone into thinking I'm a born and bred New Yorker? Check... Well, almost.*

Sophia looks down at the shiny silver duffle bag she sewed with her grandmother, who she calls Baba, over the summer. She can't wait to show Baba she's still using it.

Before she finalizes her New York City outfit selection, Sophia decides to send a quick text to her friends.

Sophia smiles at her friends' responses. She wishes she could take them with her. She first met everyone earlier this summer when they all signed up for the Passion for Fashion sewing class at Gracie Alexander-Cline's mom's store, Zoey's Closet. Well, Sophia already knew Ava Morris from school, but they didn't really become friends until they both signed up for P4F. And if it wasn't for P4F, Sophia would probably have never met Gracie, Lily Smith, or Maya Alvarez at all.

But it really feels like Sophia's known them all forever. Now that school is about to be back in session, P4F class will probably have to move to a weekday, since weekends will be packed with other classes.

Sophia takes a long look at her closet. *What else says Cool City Girl without trying too hard?* she thinks, her eyes glancing over the dozens of boxy button-downs and cropped rugby tops. *Forget it, this is too hard to do solo. I'll FaceTime Ava.*

"You called at the *perfect* time," Ava says when she appears on screen. She plops onto the plush white bed at her family's Martha's Vineyard home as Sophia sits down on the bed in her own bedroom. "I have ten minutes of downtime before my mom drives me to sailing lessons."

"You're at Martha's Vineyard and you still have lessons? You are officially the busiest human being I know," Sophia says. "Even your vacations are more packed than my regular life."

"Our trips here used to be somewhat relaxing," Ava wistfully remembers. "But not anymore. My parents decided we were wasting too much time just lounging by the pool and grabbing doughnuts in town, so now they have my brothers and me signed up for every activity this island has to offer."

"That sounds brutal," Sophia says with a shudder. "I'm sorry."

"It's not that bad," Ava replies with a smile. "Anyway, tell me about you. Are you ready for New York?"

"Mostly," Sophia says. "I just need your help picking some outfits for while I'm there."

"What about the one you made for the P4F show? You

got so many compliments on it when you wore it to lunch at Duryea's when we were in the Hamptons. Plus, you only have a few more weeks of nice weather left to wear it!"

"I didn't even think of that," Sophia says, pulling the matching crop top and shorts out of her closet. "Great idea. Then maybe I'll wear this black pin strap dress with a beige turtleneck underneath if we go out to dinner? I already packed my favorite cardigan, the one Baba knitted for me last year, but this feels like another good option for keeping warm when the AC is blasting indoors."

"Smart thinking," Ava says with a nod. "That will look so cool, especially if you pair it with boots."

As Sophia pulls the black combat boots out of her closet, her eyes catch a glimpse of the new sleeveless argyle sweater she got with her mom last weekend. "Wait, I have another idea. What if I wear a simple white tee with a pair of ripped black jeans? Then throw this sweater over the tee when we go inside? For shoes, I'll just go with a pair of chunky white sneaks."

"I think I literally saw that exact outfit in one of the NYC street-style accounts on Insta," Ava says. "You're going to look so chic."

"You're sure I won't look like I'm trying too hard?" Sophia asks, fidgeting with the soft cashmere of the sweater. "The last thing I want is to look like the suburban girl trying and failing to fit in with the city kids."

"Trust me," Ava says. "With these outfits, the city kids are going to be trying to fit in with you. What's your plan while you're there anyway?"

"First, my mom's going to take us straight to my dad's new place," Sophia says. "It's in Tribeca and my dad promises I'm going to *love* it. We tend to have the same taste, so I'm sure I will. Then he promised we're going to go shopping at some point. And I'll get to see Baba! And my old bestie, Lyla."

"Sounds incredible," Ava says. "I wish I could come!"

"I wish you could too," Sophia says. "Maybe when my dad's place is ready, we could do a P4F weekend there?"

"That would be *amazing*. I'm sure all the girls would be so in. I can't believe we're both missing the last Saturday class."

"I know," Sophia sighs. "I've gotten used to spending every single weekend with everyone. But I'm so excited to see my dad. I mean, I love my mom. Duh. But my dad and I just have a... different connection."

"I get that," Ava says with a nod. "Sometimes you just vibe with one parent more than the other. It doesn't mean you love either one more."

"Yeah, exactly," Sophia says in relief. Ava just *gets* it. "My dad and I are just into the same things, you know? He likes art and doing things outside the box. My mom likes horseback riding and being inside the box."

"You just have more in common with him," Ava says. "It's nothing to feel bad about."

"It's not just him either," Sophia continues. "I just feel more comfortable with his side of the family. I love hanging out with them and learning about their Japanese traditions."

"Where's your mom's family from again?" Ava asks. "Somewhere around here in Pennsylvania, right?"

"Yeah, my mom's mom—I call her Gigi—is from the Main Line," Sophia says. "She's just so different from Baba. Baba's all warm and cuddly and down to watch *Project Runway* with me. Gigi is kind of... set in her ways. She's always making little comments about how I dress and trying to get me to ditch fashion for a more 'appropriate' activity, like horseback riding. Sorry, I know you love horseback riding. No offense. But it's just not my thing, you know?"

"None taken," Ava says. "I love riding, but I know for a fact you would hate it. All it took was that one trip to Adventureland to prove that."

Sophia laughs, remembering the time she and the P4F girls decided to go to the amusement park's merry-go-round while they were visiting Lily's grandma in the Hamptons. Sophia could not stop complaining about how uncomfortable she was sitting atop the metal horse.

"And that was just a fake horse!" Sophia exclaims. "Imagine how I would do on a big horse that's actually real."

"You're not even factoring in the manure," Ava says. "I love my horse, Abe, but his poop *stinks*."

"Ew!" Sophia shakes her head. "Yeah, I think it's safe to say horseback riding is not for me."

"Nope. And that's fine by me. Hey, I have to go change into my sailing clothes if I'm going to make it to class on time," Ava says, fidgeting with one of the pearly white buttons on the two-tone tan and cream dress she sewed for herself a few weeks ago. "But have fun and send me pics, okay?"

"Will do," Sophia promises. "Have fun doing... I guess everything Martha's Vineyard has to offer?"

"Thanks," Ava says with a laugh. "Can't wait to swap stories when we're both back at school on Monday!"

"Same," Sophia agrees. "See ya!"

Sophia looks around her room to see if there's anything else she might want to bring before zipping her duffle up. Maybe her phone charger? She grabs the plug out of the wall and throws it into her bag, though she's pretty sure her dad probably has one waiting in New York for her.

"Soph?" Sophia can hear her mom's voice on the other side of the door. "Mind if I come in for a second?"

Sophia opens the door for her. "What's up?"

"How's the packing coming along?" her mom asks.

"It's coming. I'll be happy when Dad's finally settled and I can just keep a bunch of stuff there. I can't imagine doing this back and forth all the time."

"Understandable," her mom says. "Sorry you're missing P4F this weekend."

"Yeah, not ideal," Sophia says with a shrug. "But the girls understand. I really miss Dad, so I'm glad we're getting to see him. And Baba will be there, and we're going to go shopping and maybe get some beauty products!"

Sophia notices the look on her mom's face and instantly feels a pang of guilt. After the P4F fashion show a few weeks ago, her parents promised that they would stop fighting as much as they used to. To their credit, Sophia has been spending fewer nights falling asleep to the sound of them screaming at each other on the phone.

But having her dad living in another state doesn't feel much better. Especially when missing him automatically feels like dissing her mom. Sophia hates this. She makes one parent happy and the other a bit sad. It's like she can't win.

"Okay, I'm going to finish packing and be down in a bit!" Sophia says, trying to perk up.

"Great, babe," her mom says as she walks out. "I'll see you downstairs. Let me know if you need any help carrying everything down."

"Mom, I'm going for a weekend," Sophia says, trying not to roll her eyes. "It's one tiny duffle bag. I don't need your help."

"Tell that to your brother," her mom jokes. "I just had to convince him not to pack every single one of his *Star Wars* action figures and his chess set."

Sophia chuckles to herself as her mom shuts the door. *Classic Alan.* One time their family took a trip to Nantucket for Labor Day and Alan insisted on packing his own bedding and every single one of his toys. It's become a running joke between the four of them any time they travel anywhere. Alan treats every weekend trip like a cross-country move.

Recalling the memory is strange for Sophia. It feels like a lifetime ago that her family was a real, single unit. The divorce just happened recently, but even before that there were years of her parents fighting. Thinking of a time when they were all a happy family with inside jokes feels almost like a dream. Sophia wonders if her mom remembers the Nantucket trip and the inside joke. *Does thinking about that make her feel weird too?*

Sophia lets out a deep breath. Her first school year without her dad around is going to be tough. When she first heard that he was moving back to New York, Sophia saw it as the best of both worlds. She could have her life here with all her friends in Lower Merion, plus a bonus life with her dad in the fashion capital of America. But now that it's all becoming real, Sophia feels less optimistic about the whole thing. Without her dad around during the school week, who's going to help her with her science homework? Who's going to cheer her up when she's stressed about an exam? Who's going to make her favorite ramen soup when she has a stomachache?

"Sophia," her mom shouts from downstairs. "You ready?"

"Yes!" Sophia grabs her duffle. "Coming now!"

Slinging the bag over her shoulder, Sophia feels a buzz of excitement shoot up her spine. The time for feeling sad can come later. For now, she cannot wait to see her dad.

# two

"Here we are," Sophia's mom announces from the driver's seat of her Mercedes G Wagon. "New York City."

"Wahoo!" Alan shouts. "How much longer until we get to Dad's? We've been in this car *forever*."

"It's barely been two hours, Alan," Sophia says. "Relax." Alan does this whenever they have a car ride of any sort. Whether they're doing a trip to the grocery store or a trip across the country, Sophia's little brother wants to be at his destination as soon as he enters the vehicle.

Sophia looks out the window as their car sits in traffic on Canal Street. *I forgot how messy things are allowed to be here*, she thinks to herself, her eyes taking in all the vendors competing to sell their knockoff designer goods. Everything is so clean and perfect where she and Alan live with their mom in Lower Merion. In their neighborhood, the streets are lined with multimillion-dollar colonial homes that sit behind picket fences carefully painted the perfect shade of white. Inside those homes live hundreds of different versions of the same sort of family who sends the same sort of perfect-looking Christmas cards every year.

When they're in Lower Merion, it's like all Sophia's mom cares about is fitting in with the other families in their neighborhood. That means attending the right events, serving on the right boards, and befriending the right people. Everything is carefully curated, from the way their front lawn is landscaped to the outfits she wears for brunch at the country club. The whole thing makes Sophia's mom sort of... stiff.

But when they lived in New York, Sophia's mom could not have cared less about any of that stuff. Her parents had an eclectic group of friends in the city, and Sophia had plenty of friends whose families looked a lot like Gracie's, who has two moms. Yet on the Main Line, Gracie told Sophia that she felt

like people would look at her differently when she was out with her family. Sophia herself even noticed she was getting less invites to birthday parties from "friends" in her neighborhood since her parents split up. *Maybe Mom feels judged for the divorce too,* Sophia thinks to herself. *Maybe that's why she's been so stiff.*

But her mom is different in New York. Sophia can just tell by the smile that breaks across her mom's face the minute they make it out of Holland Tunnel. Her shoulders are totally relaxed, even though they're sitting in bumper-to-bumper traffic. New York has this effect on her mom. Something about the city reverts her back to her college days, stripping her of all the pressure feels to fit in back home on the Main Line.

Of course, there is no world in which her strict mom would ever let Sophia and Alan take the train to New York by themselves. But Sophia thinks the other reason her mom is so insistent on driving them to the city today is because she misses it herself.

"Are you happy to be back, Mom?" Sophia asks, taking in the obvious shift in her mom's energy. "I feel like you love being here."

"I really do, Soph," her mom says, rolling her window down and deeply inhaling the slightly fishy smell in the New York City air. "You know, I technically grew up in Bryn Mawr, but so much of my *real* growing up happened here when I was at NYU. It changed my life."

"But you still wound up back near where you grew up," Alan reminds her from the backseat. "Did it really change your life *that* much?"

"Sure it did," their mom says. "It's where I met your dad,

for starters. And that man *really* changed my life."

"...Like, in a good way?" Sophia asks, her voice barely audible.

"Of course," her mom replies, taking one hand off the steering wheel to give Sophia's hand a squeeze. "You see that Dunkin' Donuts on the corner there?"

Sophia and Alan both turn to look at the chain doughnut shop to their right.

"Well," their mom continues, "back in college, that was the gallery of an up-and-coming pop artist who went by the name of Spelunk. Your dad took me to see his exhibit for our second date. It took a full week for your dad to convince me to venture into this part of the city—outside of school, I spent most of my time uptown. But he finally got me to come down here and the exhibition blew my mind. I had never seen art like that before, so uninhibited and free."

Sophia was surprised that she had never heard the story before. Back when they were together, her parents were always telling her and Alan stories of their college days back

in New York, from their first date at Caffe Reggio to the time their mom dragged their dad to the annual white party at the New York Athletic Club. But once their dad moved out, those stories came to a screeching halt. Sometimes Sophia wondered if her parents even remembered any of the happy times with each other. It felt good to know the city was able to conjure up this nostalgia in her mom.

"Wow," Sophia says, Googling Spelunk on her phone. "Their stuff looks amazing. I wish I could have seen it."

"You would have loved it," her mom says, pausing for a second before adding, "And I hope you both know, even though we have our differences, which I know we have not done the best job at shielding you kids from, your father still gave me the two best things in my life. I will always be grateful to him for that."

Alan raises one eyebrow. "You mean us, right?"

"Yes, silly," their mom replies with a chuckle. "I mean you two."

Sophia didn't realize how badly she needed to hear her mom say those words. It's not like she thinks they're going to get back together or anything like that—Sophia made peace with that fact after she and Adam made a disastrous attempt to *Parent Trap* them last year. At this point, just knowing the two most important adults in her life maybe don't *totally* hate each other feels like a win.

"How would you kids feel if we grabbed drinks and a snack before going to your dad's?" her mom asks as she turns the car onto a cobblestone street. "We could try Maman. I hear their cookies are even better than Levain!"

Sophia doesn't want to shut her mom down, but she has

been looking forward to seeing her dad in person for weeks now. She just can't put it off any longer.

"Um, is it okay if you just drop us off?" Sophia asks nervously.

"Oh yeah, sure," her mom replies, clearly unbothered. "I wanted to make a quick stop at Jenni Kayne anyway for a few sweaters. No worries."

Sophia lets out a sigh of relief. "Great!"

*Now let's just hope she can maintain this chill energy when we see Dad,* Sophia thinks to herself, a knot tightening in her stomach.

# three

Sophia looks up at her dad's old brick building from where she and Alan are standing beside their mom on the sidewalk. She already loves it. Part of her wondered if her dad would have moved into one of those giant luxury buildings with the door attendants and the gyms, like the one that Lyla's dad had moved into after he and Lyla's mom split up. Not that Sophia has any issues with those sorts of buildings. They're super nice! But they just aren't right for her dad. "We like things with a little personality," he said to Sophia once.

This building has *tons* of personality. It's an adorable vine-covered brick building with a cozy coffee shop called Beth's on the ground floor. A little red door is tucked away to the left for residents to enter through. Above the front door, Sophia spots a gold plaque proclaiming this to be one of the oldest buildings in Tribeca.

*This place belongs inside of a snow globe,* Sophia thinks to herself. *It's perfect.*

"Let's take a look here," her mom says, glancing down at

her phone. "I think he said his apartment is 6B."

"I'll buzz it!" Alan exclaims. He drops his mom's hand to slam his finger on the silver button.

*Buzzers.* It has been a long time since Sophia went somewhere that has a buzzer. The loud screeching sound is definitely unpleasant, especially compared to the singsongy *ding dong* noise her doorbell makes back home. But the familiarity somehow feels refreshing, like a splash of cold water to the face.

"I think I spy my favorite people," her dad's voice booms through the intercom. "Come on up!" Another buzz sounds as he unlocks the door for them.

A wave of mixed emotions washes over Sophia as she, her mom, and Max enter her dad's building and wait for the elevator to come down. On the one hand, she is so excited she thinks she might burst. This is the longest she has ever gone without seeing her dad, and she cannot wait to run into his arms. But then there's also the lurking tension that has followed her around pretty much ever since her parents first separated. As eager as she is to see her dad, Sophia also can't help but think about the doom of an impending fight between the two adults she loves most in the world. Yes, her mom was being more civil in the car. And, yes, her parents recently promised to cut down the fighting. But the nerves Sophia built up over the past few years don't disappear that easily.

*Mom is literally in the elevator coming up to the apartment with us,* she reminds herself. *Things are different now.*

"I bet Dad's apartment is super cool," Sophia tells Alan and her mom, trying to distract herself from her nerves. "He promised I would love it."

"He said I would love it too," Alan chimes in. "Apparently my room is *filled* with all of my favorite things, so maybe he got me that life-size chess set I asked for last year for Christmas."

"Haven't you kids seen his apartment over FaceTime?" her mom asks. "You chat with him every single night. How have you not seen it yet?"

"He's tried to give us a tour a few times," Sophia says. "But the connection is always spotty and blurry."

"Yeah," Alan agrees. "Plus, he never shows us our rooms. It's supposed to be a *surprise*."

The elevator doors open into the large loft-style apartment that takes up the top two floors of the building. Sophia's jaw practically falls onto the dark hardwood floor.

"DAD," she screams as she runs into her dad's arms. The familiar scent of his Le Labo Tonka 25 cologne wraps around her. "This place is *awesome!*"

"What else did you expect from your old man?" he laughs as he gives her a tight squeeze. "I told you that you would love it."

She pulls back to look at her dad. He is so happy to see them! As he greets Alan and then her mom, Sophia looks around her dad's new home.

Even though it's in an old building, the loft looks more modern than she expected, with its dark wood floors and sleek new silver appliances. Her dad's favorite jazz station is playing over the Sonos speakers installed into the exposed brick walls throughout the apartment. Hanging on the walls are cool pieces of pop art that Sophia knows her dad must have gotten from galleries in SoHo.

*This place feels warm because it feels like him,* Sophia realizes. *It is so perfectly him.* She beams as she walks around, marveling at how the place is coming together.

Sophia makes her way back over to where her dad is standing by the elevator talking to her mom. *Please don't be fighting, please don't be fighting,* she thinks as she inches closer to them. Sophia notices her dad setting Alan down from where he had lifted him over his shoulder before greeting her mom with a hug. *That has to be a good sign, right?*

"How was the drive up here, Ainsley?" her dad asks her mom. "Any traffic?"

"Not really," her mom replies. "The drive was relatively smooth. We made great time. I was expecting it to take a bit longer."

This is a new thing Sophia has noticed they do. They just *chat*, like two cordial acquaintances who don't really know each other. It's a little awkward, but Sophia will take the slight awkwardness over a screaming match any day.

"That's great," her dad says with a nod. "You headed straight back home, or are you going to stay here for a bit?"

"I actually thought I would make a little trip of it myself," her mom replies. "I'm going to go hit the Jenni Kayne store—they're having a sale I would love to check out. Then I was thinking I might stay with Betsy while the kids are out here. You know, she's still living in the Upper East Side. I haven't properly seen her for years."

"Betsy Logan?" her dad asks.

"The one and only," her mom says with a laugh. "Remember the time she trashed her bag at that wild party you made us go to?"

"How could I forget?" her dad says with a chuckle. "We spent eight hours the next day walking up and down Canal Street trying to find an exact replica."

"No way," Sophia says, her jaw practically on the floor. "Mom, you bought a knockoff bag?!"

"And went to a wild party?!" Alan adds, before jokingly narrowing his eyes. "Who were you, lady?"

"Believe it or not, she was not *always* your strict mom," her dad says. "Ainsley Beck used to be pretty cool."

"I still am," her mom teases. "You people just don't get it."

"Sure, you are," Sophia teases back, flashes of her mom's stiff demeanor back home popping into mind. "The *coolest*."

"Okay, well... I guess I should get going," her mom says, backing toward the elevator. "I love you, kids."

"Bye, Mom!" Alan shouts from where he's plopped down by her dad's chess set in the living room.

"See you Sunday," Sophia says, already making her way over to the hallway leading to the bedrooms she's been itching to see since they arrived.

"Could I, um, maybe get a hug before I go?" her mom asks. Sophia notices her mom's eyes are adopting that reddish tinge they get right before she starts to cry.

Her dad must notice it too, because he raises his eyebrows at Sophia and nods her toward her mom.

"Your mom drove you both all the way here," her dad says. "The least you can do is give her a hug goodbye."

Sophia and Alan wrap their arms around their mom for a tight group hug.

"I love you both so much," her mom says, a singular teardrop making its way onto Sophia's shoulder. "I'll see you on Sunday, okay?"

"Yep," Sophia says. "Mom, you can relax. It's only two days!"

"You're right," her mom says, forcing a laugh as she wipes her tears away. "I'm being silly. I just… have gotten so used to having you two all to myself the past few weeks. I guess I got a bit greedy."

"They'll be back with you in no time, Ains," her dad reassures. "Now go have fun with Betsy!"

"I will," her mom says, her mood brightening at the mention of her old college friend. "I'll see you all on Sunday."

"Bye!" Alan and Sophia simultaneously say as she makes her way into the elevator.

As the doors close, Sophia feels a tinge of guilt creeping up her spine before she quickly pushes it back down. *No,* she tells herself. *This is your first weekend in New York City with Dad. There's no time to feel guilty.*

# four

"*Okay, now who is ready for the grand tour?*" Sophia's dad asks once the elevator doors have shut behind her mom.

"I am!" Sophia says, before Alan adds, "Me! Me! Me!"

"Well, it's all open concept here, which basically means I don't have any walls separating the main living areas," her dad explains. "So to the right, you probably already saw we have the kitchen."

Sophia admires the modern charcoal-colored cupboards and cement countertops. *There are no kitchens like this in Lower Merion*, she thinks to herself. *This is so cool.*

"Did you notice my fridge art?" her dad asks, gesturing to their school pictures he placed on the fridge with magnets.

"Dad, I *hate* that picture," Sophia groans. "I have lettuce in my teeth!"

"I think you look perfect." Her dad smiles. "A little lettuce in your teeth is what makes the picture exciting. Who wants a boring, old perfect school picture?"

Sophia rolls her eyes but smiles as he continues. "To the

left, you can see the living room. This is where we can do movie nights and play board games," her dad says, pointing toward a giant chocolate leather Restoration Hardware cloud sofa. Sophia takes in every single detail, from the charcoal-black cement coffee table with bronze finish at the bottom, to the silky ivory rug that looks so smooth, Sophia has to resist an urge to bury her face in it. She also loves the large white canvas hanging on the wall, covered with abstract shapes sprayed with black graffiti.

"You really crushed it," Sophia says, plopping down onto the comfortable couch. "The design is just so *you*."

"And this is a *sweet* chessboard," Alan says, gesturing toward the marble one her dad has sitting atop the coffee table.

"I'm glad you kids like," their dad says, a proud smile flashing across his face. "But we still haven't even gotten to the fun part."

"Our rooms?" Sophia leaps off the couch. "Can we *please* see them? The anticipation is very real right now!"

"If you insist, milady," her dad says, making his way out of the living area toward the hallway. "Follow me right this way."

Sophia gleefully walks behind her dad, past the many pieces of art that line his hallway toward her New York City bedroom. Every fiber of her being feels like it's about to bubble over with excitement. She has *no* idea what she is about to walk into.

Even on their blurry FaceTime calls, her dad refused to show her and Alan their rooms. "I want it to be a surprise," he told them. "I've put a lot of work into making them just right for each of you." Sophia cannot wait to see what he came up with.

"Ta-da!" her dad exclaims as he opens the third door on the right of the hallway. "Sophia Ito, may I present to you your bedroom."

Sophia walks in and her mouth drops.

The room is bigger than Sophia expected, with a beautiful modern black bed in the center and decorated with a white duvet and fluffy pillows. On the wall is a large canvas adorned with neon hearts, contrasting perfectly with the black and white colors. There is also a black desk set up by the wall, with a white sewing machine on top and a framed collage hanging above it.

"Dad," Sophia says, looking at the neon hearts. They look like they're beating as the colors flash in the light. "Are you kidding me? You went all out!"

"I tried my best," he says. "Don't mind the plain duvet. Baba and I were thinking the two of you could embroider it or something as a fun project."

"That would be amazing," Sophia says, a million design ideas already flashing across her mind.

"And if you want Ava or another one of your friends to come help you with the design, you've got plenty of space. Not only is the bed a queen, but it has a trundle underneath it that you can pull out for sleepovers."

"Yes, I can't wait to have the girls over!" Sophia squeals. "Ava is going to love this. And did you know Maya's never been to New York?"

"Then we've got to get her here immediately, if that's the case," her dad says with a smile. "There's nothing like showing someone New York City for the first time."

Sophia realizes she can't remember the last time she

showed someone New York. Actually, before this trip, she can't even really remember the last time she saw New York. Did moving to Lower Merion make her lose the New Yorker side of herself completely? How much of that little girl still exists inside of her?

She walks over to the desk in the room and peers at the piece hanging above it. "Wait, how did you get these?" Sophia asks as she spots familiar-looking pictures in the collage.

"They're all the pictures you've sent me over the summer. I thought you would like a little reminder of your life back home."

Sophia looks carefully at the pictures. It's like every single one of her favorite memories has been frozen in time forever on her wall. The shot of herself with her parents after the fashion show, the picture of her and Alan holding hands as they jumped into the pool in their backyard, the selfies she and the P4F girls took in the Hamptons, and even a shot of herself dozing off on Baba's shoulder while they caught up on *Project Runway* reruns.

Sophia looks down at the desk and immediately recognizes the Brother Project Runway sewing machine she spent the past year begging her parents for. "No way! You actually got it?! Dad, you are the best!"

"It was the *least* I could do," he says, pulling back the light gray velvet curtains to the right of her desk to reveal a view of a small park behind their building.

Sophia gazes out at the tiny little park filled with kids playing tag and moms chatting by the roses that line its borders. "And I get a view?" She grins. "You're seriously spoiling me."

"You *seriously* are," Alan chimes in. "My room better be this cool!"

"I have a feeling you'll be pleased with it," their dad tells Alan, giving him a light noogie on his head. "Let me just show Soph one more thing before we head over to yours."

"What more could there possibly be?" Sophia asks, following as her dad makes his way over to the door to the right of her desk. "This is already pretty much the best room ever."

"Well, would it make it even better if you had your own bathroom?" her dad asks, slowly opening the door. "Because you do."

"This is too good to be true," Sophia squeals. "No more fighting with Alan for the shower!"

"Thank the *lord*," Alan sighs.

Sophia opens the drawers under the sink and sees it has been fully stocked with all her beauty needs. "Did Baba have something to do with this?" Sophia asks, pulling her favorite Korean face cream out of one of the drawers.

"Yep," her dad says with a nod. "She wanted to make sure her favorite granddaughter was set up with all her favorite products."

"Baba knows me so well," Sophia says with a grin. "Where is she anyway?"

"She's out for lunch with some friends right now," he says. "But don't worry. You will get plenty of Baba time later."

"Okay, *now* can we see my room?" Alan asks.

"You've got it, bud," their dad replies, making his way out of Sophia's bathroom. "Right this way."

Alan and Sophia follow their dad back into the hallway

where they find Alan's room next to Sophia's.

"This is awesome!" Alan yelps as he bursts through the door. "A race car bed? Dinosaur sheets? A table just for playing chess?"

"Just wait until you see *this*," their dad says, shutting the lights off. "Check out your chess set now."

"No way," Alan says, his voice barely audible. "It glows in the dark?!"

"Alan, look up!" Sophia says, her eyes catching a glimpse of the full constellation of glow-in-the-dark stars their dad tacked onto the ceiling.

"These might be a nice solution for if you get a little scared of the dark," their dad tells Alan. "What do you think?"

"Best solution ever," Alan says, his jaw still practically on the floor as their dad turns the lights back on.

"All right, now that everyone has seen their bedrooms, what do you say we pick where we're going to head out today?"

"Sure!" Sophia says, excited to see what her dad has in mind.

"So, I definitely think we should check out a museum," he says. "The question is which one. Sophia, I thought you would enjoy the Met to see the fashion from the Met Gala exhibit before it shuts down. Alan, while we're there, we could also check out an exhibit they have on Disney that sounds pretty neat."

"Hmm," Alan ponders. "What are our other options?"

"What do you mean what are our other options? The Met is obviously the only option," Sophia says. "We all know I love fashion. And Alan, you love Disney! It's a win-win."

"The other option is the Museum of Natural History,"

their dad says. "They have some cool dinosaurs for Alan to check out *and* they have an exhibit on Japanese culture I have a feeling you would be super into, Soph. What do you think?"

"That does sound pretty cool," Sophia concedes. "But the Met Gala exhibit is gonna close any day now. Can we check out the Met this weekend then next weekend do the Museum of Natural History?"

"If Alan's in, so am I," their dad says, turning his attention toward Alan.

"I guess that works," Alan says with a shrug. "But only because we all know I'm the bigger person in this siblinghood."

"Sure you are," Sophia says, rolling her eyes before letting out a laugh.

Being bored in New York simply isn't an option like it is back in Lower Merion. Before she signed up for classes at Zoey's Closet, Sophia's Saturdays at home pretty much just consisted of hanging at her house or riding her bike over to a friend's house. Sure, she would have loved to go to an exhibit to learn more about her family's heritage or about the highest of high fashion. But that's simply not an option there. Here, *everything* is an option.

# five

Sophia can hardly contain her excitement to look through all the different outfits Anna Wintour and her team curated for the theme of this year's Met Gala exhibit, "Darkness to Light."

So, while her dad helps Alan unpack his bags in his room, Sophia takes her own crack at making a "Darkness to Light" outfit using the clothes she packed for the weekend. After careful examination, she decides to go with the black pin strap dress and combat boots. But instead of pairing the dress with the beige turtleneck underneath, Sophia opts for a crisp white T-shirt. *I'll bring my cardigan in case I get cold at the museum,* she resolves. *It's too hot outside to be walking around in long sleeves.*

After putting the full outfit on, she takes a photo of herself using the full-length mirror her dad mounted on her bathroom door and sends it to the P4F group text.

**P4F** 💬 & 🎵

TODAY

I feel like the tee gives it a little more of a daytime vibe. Plus, it's more of a crisp white, so it really highlights the theme, don't you guys think?

**Ava**
Totally

**Ava**
You're giving me major Bella Hadid energy

Sophia feels her confidence soar with the flood of nice texts from her friends.

Once ready, she, Alan, and her dad make their way uptown to the Met, reminding Sophia of the good old days when traveling here was almost a weekly occurrence. Excitedly, her eyes move rapidly around the rooms as they walk through the museum until they reach the exhibit.

Sophia can hardly believe the designs she is seeing. Of course she gobbled up all the celebrity looks from the Met Gala from photos online. But seeing the actual exhibit in person is something else entirely. The theme is simple, but every designer has their own unique take on it.

"What do you think of this one, Soph?" Her dad gestures her over to a mannequin dressed in high-waisted black pants and a fitted shirt in the brightest shade of neon green Sophia has ever seen. "It's simple, but it feels like it's still got some excitement, don't you think?"

"Oh my gosh," Sophia says, snapping a picture of the look. "It is so Lily. She is going to love this look."

"Lily is the one with the classic, simple style, right? The one who made the jumpsuit for the charity fashion show?"

Sophia nods, remembering the iconic jumpsuit Lily created. "Yep. Did I tell you she made that based on an old picture of her mom?"

"You did," her dad says. "What a special way to honor her mom's memory."

"Yeah," Sophia agrees. "It meant a lot to Lily."

"My favorite thing about fashion is learning the story behind the design," her dad says. "Like this look, for example. The designer's statement says she created it as a representation of the hope that kept her going in her darkest hours as a Syrian refugee. Without knowing that, I would just think it's a beautiful outfit. But if I dig deeper, every design has a story."

As Sophia continues looking around the exhibit, she snaps pictures of everything that reminds her of her P4F pals. *Lily would be so into these,* Sophie thinks as she takes shots of a bright-white satin slip wedding gown and an impeccably fitted black power suit with the gigantic wide-leg pants. For Gracie, she finds a gothic-looking black lace gown with the silver metal spikes jutting out of the shoulders, though it's the bubblegum-pink satin gown with the words *PUNK IS LIFE* splattered across the front in black paint that really stands out. *It matches Gracie's pink hair,* Sophia thinks. For Maya, Sophia snaps shots of an ombré denim jumpsuit that's got a bit of Southern flair, plus a gown a designer created using real flowers that start white at the top and gradually become a dark burgundy as they trail down the dress.

When it comes to taking pictures for Ava, there are almost too many outfits to choose from. Ava loves a nice, fitted, feminine dress, and this exhibit is filled with them. Sophia snaps picture after picture for her bestie, one of a black gown adorned with tiny white flowers, another of a navy silk suit trimmed with aqua-colored feathers at the sleeves. The one Sophia knows Ava would love most is a gorgeous yellow gown with a massive train that somehow manages to embody the color of sunshine.

As for her own personal inspiration, Sophia finds herself drawn to the zanier outfits: a dress created entirely out of lightbulbs; a black dress embroidered with glow-in-the-dark thread spelling out *I LOVE YOU* in cursive. Finally, she finds herself standing in front of a beautiful white taffeta gown that the designer hired a street artist to cover in black graffiti. For a moment, she stands there, transfixed.

"This one's my favorite," her dad says, coming up from behind her. "You can just *feel* the passion the designer put into creating this."

Sophia grabs her dad's hand and gives it a squeeze as they both take in the gown. There is something special about having a dad who really *gets* her. And not in a trying-to-be-nice-and-supportive way. His mind just works the same way hers does. Their hearts skip a beat for the same things. Not everyone has this sort of connection with *anybody*, let alone their own parent.

After the museum, they go to dinner at Serendipity, where a familiar face is already waiting for them at a table. "Baba!" Sophia exclaims running through the pink restaurant toward her beloved grandmother. "I missed you so much."

"Hi, sweetie," Baba says, giving her a tight hug and a kiss atop her head. "I missed you right back."

"Hey, what am I, chopped liver?" Alan jokes as he makes his way over. "Where's my hug?"

"My favorite boy," Baba coos, letting out her signature hearty laugh. "Of course you get a hug."

"Okaasan," their dad says, giving Baba a hug before he takes his seat across the table from her. "We missed you at the Met Gala exhibit today."

"Yeah, it was pretty cool," Alan says. "The Disney exhibit was cooler. But the fashion wasn't as boring as I thought it would be."

"Baba, look at this dress that was Dad's and my favorite," Sophia says, pulling up the picture of the white taffeta gown to show Baba. "Is it not the best take on 'Darkness to Light' you could ever imagine?"

"Let me see," Baba says, putting her glasses on as she examines the dress. "Very nice. Sophia, I was thinking we could maybe do something similar for your duvet. What do you say we cover it in spray paint? I already bought some at the store if you're interested."

"Yes, yes, yes," Sophia says, clapping her hands with excitement. "I've never spray painted anything before. Have you?"

"This is going to be a first for both of us," Baba says with a smile. "I have a feeling we will be making some mistakes, and you know what I always say about those..."

"If you're not making mistakes, you're not having fun," Sophia recites back her grandma's favorite line, already looking forward to laughing off whatever goes wrong with

Baba by her side.

Baba nods. "Now, I hope you don't mind, but I already went ahead and placed a few orders for the table. Alan, I know you can't say no to their chicken tenders. Sophia, I got the wagyu sliders just for you."

"Yum," Sophia says, her mouth salivating at just the thought of the dish she enjoyed so many times growing up.

"So, what did you kids think about your dad's new place?" Baba asks. "Pretty nice, right?"

"The décor could not have been better," Sophia says. "Dad, where did you get all that art anyway?"

"Oh, I went to so many galleries in Soho," he says with a laugh. "I visited at least a dozen before I started narrowing down on my favorite pieces. Some of them are the real deal. I'm still thinking I need one more piece for the hallway. Maybe an Alec Monopoly, but those are pretty pricy."

"An Alec Monopoly would be *awesome*," Sophia says, remembering a painted wall of his that she saw during a family trip to Miami a few years ago. "His stuff is so cool."

"Monopoly?" Alec asks, an eyebrow raised. "Like the game?"

"Sort of," Sophia explains. "He's an artist and uses the Monopoly man as his symbol in his art."

"I like Monopoly," Alan says. "Count me as a fan."

As Alan and their dad start talking about chess, Baba turns to Sophia. "How's Passion for Fashion? Are you sad you're missing class to be here today?"

"Yeah, I miss my friends," Sophia says, taking a bite of her slider as soon as the waitress sets the plate down on their table. "But being back in the city has been so nice. Not to mention seeing you and Dad. I know it hasn't even been that long, but I really missed you both."

"I missed you too, honey," Baba replies. "Watching *Project Runway* is not the same without my Sophia."

By the time Sophia has the last bite of her favorite Unicorn Bliss Sundae, she feels totally caught up on her dad and Baba's new lives here in New York. She knows all about the girlfriends Baba reconnected with since moving back and the new Japanese market she's been shopping at. And Sophia's fully up to speed on her dad's new job, how it's demanding but not quite as stressful as his last job.

*I can't believe how much can change in just a few weeks,* Sophia thinks to herself, her chest then tightening at the thought that she's going to have to leave her dad and Baba again in just twenty-four hours.

# six

"So, this is the one, huh?" Sophia's dad asks, picking up the special edition gold Fjällräven backpack Sophia's been eyeing the whole summer. "The famous 'must have' backpack?"

Sophia's mom will be picking her and Alan up in just a few hours, but her dad was determined to make the most of their last few hours together. So, the three of them headed out for a little shopping trip to SoHo.

"Yep," Sophia nervously says, hoping her dad loves it as much as she does. "I'm almost starstruck seeing it in person."

"*Starstruck*?" Alan scoffs. "C'mon, it's a bag!"

"Hey," Sophia fires back at her brother sternly. "I didn't make any rude comments when you got heart eyes over chess sets at Chess Forum. Let me have this."

"She's got a point, bud," their dad says. "We let you have your thing. Now let's give your sister her thing."

"Fine," Alan says. "You can be starstruck by a backpack if I can be starstruck by a chess set. Sorry."

"Apology accepted," Sophia tells her little brother, before shooting her dad a grateful smile. It feels good having someone take her side, especially when she feels like her mom is always taking Alan's side back at home. If she were here, Sophia knows exactly what she would say: *Sophia, he's younger than you. Rise above it.*

"Soph, I have to admit, I did not love the backpack in the pictures you sent me," her dad says, carefully examining the backpack like he's a cardiologist and it's a beating heart. "But this might be the most perfectly crafted backpack I've ever seen."

"You think?" Sophia asks, her entire body perking up. "Really?"

"Really," her dad says, giving her a quick peck on the forehead. "And I think it would be a crime to let you walk into Charis without it slung over your shoulder for the first day."

"So… you're getting me the backpack?" Sophia is in disbelief that this key element of her back-to-school vision board might actually be coming to life.

"I'm getting you the backpack," her dad confirms. "And

whenever you use it at school, I want you to think of this special day."

"I will," Sophia says, wrapping her arms around him for the tightest hug she can muster. "You are the BEST."

Once they check out at the Fjällräven store, Sophia, her dad, and Alan head to Sadelle's where they're meeting one of Sophia's oldest NYC besties, Lyla, along with Lyla's mom and her little brother, Seth, for brunch.

Lyla and her family are seated in the back of the restaurant, but Sophia spots her old friend as soon as she enters. To be fair, Lyla's hard to miss. She has jet-black hair, and she's always dyeing the front a different bright color. Today, it's an aquamarine color that almost exactly matches her strikingly bright eyes. *Kind of like Gracie's pink hair,* Sophia thinks. *I bet Gracie and Lyla would get along great.*

"Sophster!" Lyla shouts, jumping out of her seat as soon as she spots Sophia walking toward their table.

Sophia giggles at the childhood nickname. Though she would probably cringe if anyone else called her that now, it feels good coming from her old friend.

"Hey, Lyle!" Sophia says, giving her a big hug. Sophia takes in the matching colorful silk patchwork short-sleeve button down and shorts Lyla has paired with a fringed brown suede jacket. "Your outfit is awesome."

"Thanks, girl," Lyla says, doing a little twirl. "I found the whole look thrifting at 10 ft Single."

"The thrift shop in Brooklyn?" Sophia asks, instantly recognizing it the name. "According to TikTok, that's where all my favorite celebrities find their best looks."

"Yeah!" Lyla confirms. "I find all my coolest pieces there."

"I've always wanted to go," Sophia says. "The thrift shops around me in Pennsylvania never have anything that cool."

"I guess that's just another reason you have to come back here more often, right?"

"I guess so," Sophia says. She takes a seat across from Lyla at the end of the table so they can properly catch up.

"So, how is it?" Lyla asks in a low voice. "Any better than before?"

Sophia doesn't even have to ask to know that Lyla's referring to Sophia's parents' divorce. Though they text about it all the time, this is Sophia's first time actually seeing Lyla in

person since her parents split up.

"It's getting less awful, I guess," Sophia says quietly. "Like, this weekend has been great. But then I think about having to go back to Lower Merion and being away from my dad and Baba... and it just makes me kind of sad, you know?"

Lyla nods. "I get it. I mean, my dad just moved to the Upper West Side. But having a parent uptown and a parent downtown might as well be like having parents in different states."

Sophia lets out a laugh. She knows exactly what Lyla means. Sometimes New York can feel so big because traveling from one place to another seems to take forever.

"But you said they aren't fighting as much anymore, right?" Lyla asks.

"Yeah," Sophia confirms, taking a piece of lox off the tower the server just placed between them and putting it on top of her everything bagel. "I did this fashion show thing with some of my friends from home, and after that my mom and dad promised they would cut down on the fighting around us. It is *super* awkward watching them interact sometimes, but at least they're trying."

"You're lucky," Lyla says, keeping her voice low so her mom, who is talking to Sophia's dad at the other end of the table, can't hear. "My parents don't even *try*. It's been three years and I still hear them yelling at each other on the phone every other night."

"I don't know how you handle it," Sophia says. "The yelling is the worst. But, I don't know... having them so far apart has been tough in new ways."

"Are you always just missing one of them?" Lyla asks,

spreading some scallion cream cheese onto her bagel. "That happens to me a lot."

"Yeah, but it's not even just missing one of them," Sophia says. "It's missing the lives I have with them both. This weekend has been so fun, and I know as soon as I go back, I'm going to wish I could be here having brunch with you and checking out cool museum exhibits. But then while I'm here, I'm thinking about my friends from home and my sewing class that I had to miss."

"I know it doesn't seem this way, but you get used to it," Lyla says. "Trust me, I've been there."

"Thanks, Lyle," Sophia says, her eyes getting glassy again. Sophia loves her friends at home, but none of their parents are divorced. They're there for her when she gets sad about divorce stuff, but they don't really get it the way Lyla gets it. Lyla's parents divorced a few years ago so she's used to all of this. Instead of reacting to Sophia's stories with pity, Lyla casually nods as if this is all just par for the course. Lyla makes Sophia feel like maybe her problems aren't so unique after all.

"Anyway, Sophster, you still have the best style," Lyla says. "Where did you get that sweater?"

"I got it with my mom at a boutique near my house a few weeks ago," Sophia says, perking up as she looks down. She layered her argyle sweater over a white tee and ripped jeans.

"You crush that preppy but edgy look," Lyla says. "I keep showing your Instagram posts to my friends for fashion inspo."

"Really?" Sophia asks, her face turning bright red. "I feel like I don't dress anywhere near cool enough for New York City. I was so stressed about what to pack for this weekend."

"What are you talking about?" Lyla says, taking a latka from one of the side plates and dunking it into applesauce. "You're a born and bred New Yorker!"

"I guess I forget that sometimes," Sophia says. "I've been away from the city for so long."

"Well, now you're back. It feels right, doesn't it?"

Sophia nods. *It really does.*

"You should start leaving some clothes here instead of bringing them back and forth between your dad's and your mom's," Lyla says. "Pro tip, from one child of divorce to another—having two closets is one of the perks! Don't pass it up."

The girls agree that the next time Sophia comes, they will work on getting her New York closet organized. Sophia finds herself immediately counting the days to when that will be. It cannot come soon enough.

# seven

$S$*ophia readjusts her too-tight headband and sighs. In just a few hours she has gone from New York chic to... this.*

Her mom insisted they all dress up tonight for their first family dinner back at home in Lower Merion, which means wearing outfits she picks out for Sophia and Alan. For Sophia, it's this uncomfortable white headband paired with a brightly patterned pink-and-green Lily Pulitzer dress she hasn't worn since Gigi's Memorial Day party last summer. For his part, Alan is wearing a turquoise Ralph Lauren button-down shirt and a pair of slacks.

Normally, Sophia would insist on wearing something with a little more edge. But she just isn't up for the fight tonight.

"Sophia, do you want some more spinach or

mashed potatoes?" her mom asks from across the dinner table. "You barely touched your chicken."

"I'm good," Sophia replies, poking her fork at the piece of chicken breast on her plate. "I think I'm still stuffed from the bagel and latkas at Sadelle's."

"That was hours ago," Sophia's mom says, her brows furrowed with concern. "Is it the chicken? I can make you something else. Maybe some salmon? We've got some leftover in the fridge that I could heat up real quick."

"No, it's okay," Sophia says. "I'm just not hungry. Really."

The chicken *is* a little bland, but the truth is Sophia probably would not be touching her plate even if it was her favorite rigatoni with spicy vodka sauce from Carbone. She just doesn't have much of an appetite tonight. Ever since she had to say bye to her dad and Baba a few hours ago, she's been feeling sort of... off.

"Okay," her mom says with a shrug. "Suit yourself. Anyway, as I was saying, Jodie was supposed to co-chair the ladies golf outing with me. But then she dropped out at the last minute. Can you believe that? It's like nobody values their commitments these days."

"*People*," Alan sighs as he gobbles up his third helping of mashed potatoes. His white linen napkin is tucked into his shirt to avoid any potential stains. "Can't live with them, can't live without them."

"Seriously," her mom agrees, letting out a little chuckle at Alan's too-mature-for-his-age comment. "So, I've been thinking a lot about what I'm going to do. First, I asked Gigi to replace Jodie with someone else. But you kids know your Gigi. She's so busy with a million other events she's working on.

And then it hit me—Genevieve Sullivan! The last time I saw her at the club, she mentioned she wanted to get involved..."

Sophia does her best to nod along, but she's barely processed a word. Her mom has been going on about this golf thing she's co-chairing at her country club later this month for what feels like hours. She knows she should be listening and wants to care about what her mom has to say, but golf outings just aren't Sophia's jam. Sophia has ridden around in the golf cart with her mom and Gigi at more than a few of these things and they all feel sort of stuffy and fake, like a bunch of the mean girls at her school grew up and decided to hit the links together.

"...her husband is in politics, so she has tons of experience hosting fundraising events for him. Obviously, this is a different sort of event, but I think she will be a huge *asset*. I am really thrilled about the idea..."

53

As her mom talks, Sophia looks around their home, with its large windows and all-white decor. When they first moved into this house from the city, Sophia thought it was the coolest place in the world. She and her dad spent hours trying to source the perfect furniture to fit their aesthetic. Every piece of furniture, from the white boucle couch in their living room to the white marble table she, her mom, and Alan are sitting around now, sparks a special memory for Sophia.

Then she thinks about her P4F friends and how fun this past summer has been with them. *They're, like, one of the best things about Lower Merion*, Sophia thinks to herself. And, even if they don't always see eye to eye, of course she loves her mom, who is here.

But then Sophia can't help but think about her incredible room at her dad's apartment, with her new sewing machine and the duvet cover she's going to work on with Baba. She thinks about hanging with Lyla, walking around the busy streets, and finding endless options of things to do.

*Both my lives at home and New York are pretty great*, Sophia thinks to herself. *So why do I feel so... weird?*

"...as far as tablescapes for the after-golf luncheon go," her mom continues. "I'm a little worried it's cliche, but I was thinking white orchids—"

"Mom, can I go to Ava's?" Sophia interjects, the words bursting out of her mouth before she's even had a chance to think them through. Ava lives close by and they often go over to each other's house. *Ava will know how to make this better*, Sophia thinks to herself. *Ava knows how to make everything better.*

"Honey, it's after eight and you have school tomorrow,"

Sophia's mom responds. "Maybe tomorrow?"

Sophia lets out a sigh. Tomorrow sounds nice, but she needs to connect with Ava sooner than that. "Can I at least video chat with her?"

"Sure," her mom says. "That should be fine."

"Great!" Sophia perks up as she grabs her dish from the table.

"Oh... I wasn't expecting you to get up right now," her mom says, her eyes following Sophia as she makes her way over to the dishwasher. "You don't want to hear more about the golf outing?"

"Maybe later?" Sophia suggests as she clears her plate and places it into the bottom rack of the dishwasher. "I'm in desperate need for some Ava time."

"Okay, sweetie," her mom says. "Enjoy."

Her mom seems a little bummed to see Sophia getting up so abruptly, but Sophia tells herself she can follow up about the golf event tomorrow. For now, she needs to catch up with her BFF.

*Mom has friends too*, Sophia reminds herself as she moves toward her bedroom. *She gets it.*

Shutting the bedroom door behind her, Sophia rips off her formal attire, throws on her baggy linen pinstripe button-down pajamas, and plops on top of the bed that her mom forced her to make before heading off to New York.

Sophia looks at the time: 8:45 p.m. Most people would not be busy at this hour the night before the first day of school, but Ava is not most people. She has the most packed schedule Sophia has ever seen. Sophia decides to shoot her a text before FaceTiming her.

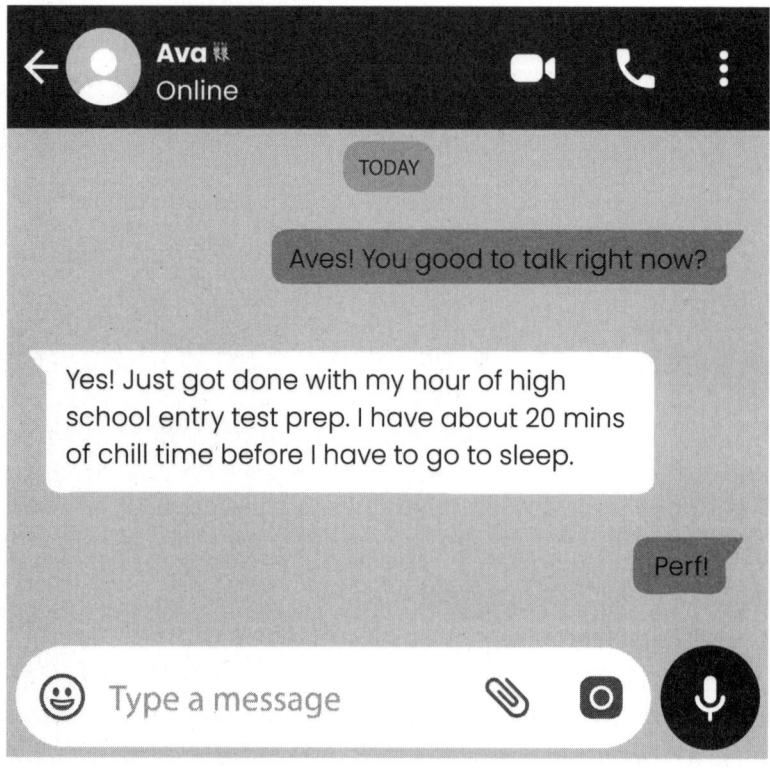

Before Sophia knows it, her bestie's face is on the phone screen.

"How was Martha's Vineyard?" Sophia asks.

"I think I need a vacation from that vacation," Ava jokes. "The schedule my parents had us on was so intense."

"Ugh, that's such a bummer," Sophia says, noticing the clear goo Ava has spread all over her face. "But you look pretty chill now. Is that the new Sunday Riley face mask? I hear it's basically magic."

"Yep," Ava replies. "I have three zits that need to be evicted from my face by morning. Can you believe tomorrow we'll officially be seventh graders?"

"No!" Sophia says. "I was trying to work on some patches for my Jordans, but they won't be ready in time. But guess what."

"What?" Ava asks. "Don't tell me it's the backpack."

"It's the backpack!" Sophia gleefully confirms, turning the camera toward the gold Fjällräven backpack sitting on her desk. "My dad got it for me while we were shopping in Soho."

"Shut *up*!" Ava squeals. "Oh my gosh, it looks even better on screen than it does on the website."

"Just wait until you see it in person," Sophia says. "The material is so soft. I want to see if I can find something like it to sew with."

"Did you finish your artistic response to *The Hate U Give*? I'm still so bummed we don't have English together."

"I know, same. Having a class together would have been so fun," Sophia says. "I can't believe you've had your response done for so long. I just finished mine on Friday because my mom said I can't go to New York until it's done."

Sophia worked hard on her artistic response too. To visually depict the book's themes, she printed out pictures of people enjoying predominantly white parties and contrasted them with pictures of people marching in Black Lives Matter protests across the country. The book had a powerful impact on Sophia, especially considering she goes to a predominantly white private school and her best friend Ava is Black. "I wish we could do collages instead of papers every time. It's not always easy for me to get my point across in a book report, but making a collage feels so much more natural."

"Agreed," Ava says, nodding. "I would *way* rather do an artistic response than a book report. Especially when we

already have to do seven other book reports. But you should have seen the look on my dad's face when he asked why I was doing arts and crafts in the living room and I told him it was for homework. Truly priceless."

Sophia laughs along with Ava. Ava's parents are many things, but artsy is not one of them.

"So, how's being back from New York? Was it amazing?" Ava asks.

"Yeah, it was awesome," Sophia says, her stomach still churning. "I don't know why, but I've just felt sort of out of it ever since I got back here."

"Didn't you get back, like, three hours ago?" Ava asks, jokingly checking her Apple watch.

"Yeah, I guess I did *just* get back," Sophia says, the knots in her stomach slowly untangling at the realization. "Maybe this feeling will go away by tomorrow."

"I'm *sure* it will," Ava says. "Plus, tomorrow is the first day of school! Are you still down to sit with me at my table for lunch? I already told the girls and they're so excited. They thought you were so fun at Isabella's pool party."

Sophia would never say it to her, but Ava's friends sort of rubbed Sophia the wrong way at that party. Sophia noticed a few of them side-texting mean things about each other at different points throughout the day. But Sophia has never really had a formal "crew" to eat lunch with at Charis, and now that she and Ava are so close, it only makes sense she would sit with Ava and her friends.

"Totally," Sophia tells Ava, the knots in her stomach starting to form again.

"Cool," Ava says. "Now go get some sleep. Studies show we need at *least* nine hours for optimal brain function."

But after Sophia hangs up, she stays on her phone. She knows Ava is right and that her mom will probably be at her door in a few minutes to regurgitate the same information, but she wants to send Lyla a quick text before calling it a night.

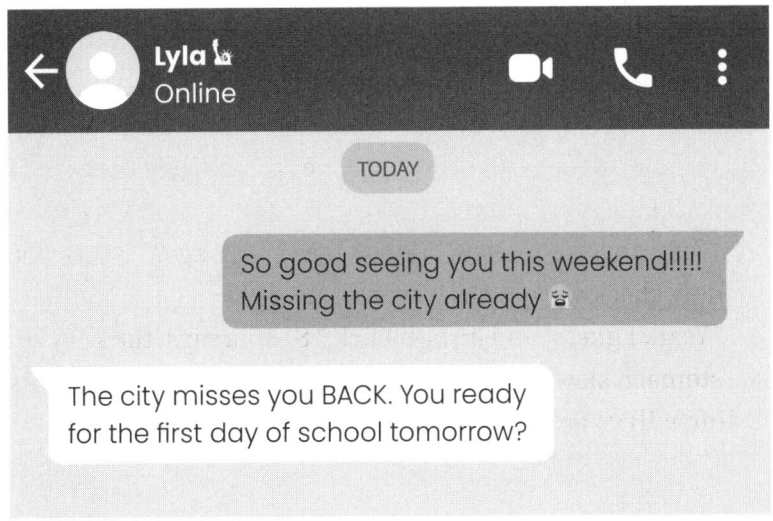

> Yep. Kinda nervous... I've been going to Charis ever since we moved here, but I'm always a little nervous the day before.

Totally know what you mean. I get nervous every year the night before too. And I'm sleeping at my dad's new place, which means tomorrow I have to go to school using another subway line. It throws off my morning routine!!!!

> First days are scary enough, I can't imagine having the subway involved!

I can't believe suburb kids just get to have their parents drive them. So lucky!

Sometimes we take the bus or ride our bikes. But those are both pretty easy. The subway is cool tho! I bet you see the coolest fashion on there

OMG one time I saw Dua Lipa on our way to school in the morning. It was epic!

> That is amazing!!!!!!!!!!!!

> OK, gotta go to bed before my mom comes and tells me to get off my phone

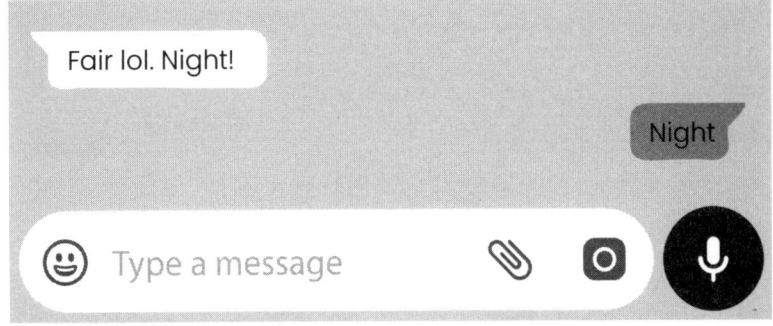

Sophia plugs her phone into the charger on her nightstand, tucks herself under her covers, and switches off the one light she had on next to her bed.

"Night, Mom!" she shouts as loud as she can so her mom knows she's actually going to sleep.

"Night, Soph!" her mom calls back. "Sleep tight!"

Sophia closes her eyes and tries to imagine school tomorrow. New teachers, new classes, new schedules. Even lunch will feel different. Even though they have gone to school with each other for years, Sophia and Ava didn't become close friends before P4F class brought them together this summer. If anything, Sophia was a little intimidated by Ava. She and her friends are the most popular girls at Charis and, while Sophia wouldn't really call herself an outcast, she's usually a little more under the radar at school. She wonders what hanging with all those girls at school will be like.

# eight

*Sophia gives her outfit one last look in the* little mirror she taped onto her locker door. *I mean, at least I like it,* she thinks nervously to herself.

The uniforms at Charis can be a little stifling in the creativity department, but Sophia likes to think of them as a challenge. How can she take the classically preppy navy blazer, white button-down, and pleated skirt, and give the outfit a bit of her signature edge? Today, she manages to pull it off with the gold backpack, a few chunky silver and gold link bracelets she bought from a street vendor in Soho, and her white Jordans. She originally planned to sew metallic patches onto the shoes, but she has to admit the unfinished look may even be a bit cooler.

Shutting the locker door, Sophia looks down her iPad one more time to double-check her schedule. The last thing she wants to do is be the one to stumble into the wrong classroom on the first day of school. The embarrassing thought sends a shiver up her spine.

*Yep*, she thinks to herself as she carefully examines the tablet with all her classes. *Homeroom in Room 37A with Ms. Benoir.*

After years at Charis, Sophia knows pretty much all the teachers here, so Ms. Benoir must be new. Sophia takes a deep breath and opens the door to the classroom.

"Bonjour," a young woman dressed in a structured white dress covered in black polka dots says as Sophia enters the classroom. "I'm Ms. Benoir. I just moved here from Paris and I am delighted to meet you. In addition to being here for homeroom, I will also be teaching history this year."

"Hi, Ms. Benoir," Sophia says, instantly liking her chic Parisian teacher. "I'm Sophia."

"Sophia Ito?" Ms. Benoir looks down at something on her desk. "Yes, the only Sophia in our class. Lovely. I have you sitting in the front here."

Sophia turns and her face instantly flashes a bright shade of red when she notices who is sitting in the desk next to hers. Sophia has had a crush on Ryan Williams for as long as she can remember, and things sort of escalated between them in the summer when he asked her to be his girlfriend. They mostly just FaceTimed and Snapchatted a lot, and Ryan even wrote a couple of songs on his guitar for her. But Sophia's parents have a strict no-boyfriend rule, so when they found out about him, they grounded Sophia for two weeks and made her break up with him immediately.

At the time, it felt extremely dramatic and unfair. But now Sophia sort of gets where her parents are coming from. There's no need to rush into boyfriends. She can do all of that when she gets to high school in a couple years. Plus, when

she broke things off with Ryan, she found she had way more time to focus on doing other things, like sewing and hanging with her friends. Actually, seeing him in front of her right now just makes Sophia realize how little she had thought about him recently.

But seeing him also reminds her that she really liked him a lot. Hence the blushing.

"Hey, Soph," Ryan says, his bright blue eyes looking up at her as Ms. Benoir greets another student. "Or, um, can I still call you that?"

"Yeah," she says with a nervous giggle as she slides into her own desk next to his. "You don't have to be my *boyfriend* to call me by my nickname."

"Well, good," he says, letting out a little sigh of relief. "Because I always liked calling you that."

"Right," Sophia says, her voice shaking a little more than

she would like it to. "So, um, Soph it is."

"Soph it is," Ryan echoes, his mouth curling upward into an adorable smile.

Sophia tries her best to stop blushing as Ms. Benoir clears her throat to kick off their very first homeroom.

The morning flies by. It turns out Sophia's one of five students in homeroom to have Ms. Benoir for history next period, so they stay put as the rest of their classmates from homeroom shuffle out. Sophia relaxes a bit in her seat. She has never considered herself much of a history buff, but Ms. Benoir's description of the Byzantine empire is so gripping that by the end of it, Sophia almost forgets about Ryan flashing her that smile.

But in third period Sophia sees him again in Mr. Wilfred's English class. After Sophia presents her collage, Ryan gives her a quick fist bump. By fourth-period biology with Mr. Levy, Sophia's stomach is grumbling for lunch. *I guess my appetite is back*, she thinks to herself. *Maybe Ava was right. I just needed some time to adjust to being back home.*

As Sophia shuffles out of Mr. Levy's classroom, she sees Ava standing by what must be her locker across the hall.

"Aves!" Sophia shouts across the busy hall. "Hi!"

"Soph!" Ava squeals, giving her a squeeze. "I can't believe we haven't seen each other all day."

"I know," Sophia says with a sigh. "This day flew by. I feel like my mom just dropped me off twenty minutes ago."

"Are you feeling better now?" Ava asks, furrowing her brows with concern. "You seemed pretty down last night."

Sophia nods. "I think you were right. I just needed some time to adjust."

"I knew it," Ava says, a big smile flashing across her face. "Besides, I don't know how anyone would have time to think of anything else with how intense these classes are. I knew seventh grade was going to be tough, but how do I already have four hours of homework lined up for tonight? *Plus* I need to start thinking of ideas for my final presentation."

"What?" Sophia asks, shocked her friend is already thinking about the project each seventh grader is supposed to submit at the end of the school year in June. "You're already thinking about final presentations?"

"I know, but if I worry now, I can *mitigate* my stress for later," Ava says. "That's why I'm always trying to get ahead."

"Huh," Sophia says. "I guess I'm just more of a 'relax now so I can stress later' kind of girl. But then again, I'm not in all the advanced classes like you are. You probably have lots of extra work on your plate."

"It's definitely not going to be a facile year, I can tell you that much," Ava says.

Sophia gives her a confused look and Ava adds, "Facile means 'easy.' My high school entrance exam tutor told me the best way to nail down the vocab is to start using it in daily conversations."

"Got it," Sophia says with a grin. "Hey, I love your twist on the uniforms today. It looks so good, Aves."

Her friend really does look incredible. Something about the exact shade of camel Ava chose for her scarf and shoes perfectly complements the dark navy of their uniforms.

"So does yours!" Ava looks Sophia up and down. "If I were to describe your look in vocab words, I would go with arresting yet perennial."

"Thanks, I guess?" Sophia laughs, making a mental note to look both those words up later.

"Hey, Aves," Isabella Rossi drawls, staring at her phone as she slowly makes her way over to where Sophia and Ava are standing. Charis doesn't allow students to be on their cell phones during school hours, but Isabella's parents are huge donors to the school, which means Isabella can get away with pretty much whatever she wants. "You ready for lunch?"

Sophia stands up straight. Isabella has been Ava's very best friend since kindergarten and has been nothing but nice to Sophia—she even welcomed her over her house for that pool party over the summer! But something about her and the rest of Ava's crew at school just gives Sophia a bad gut feeling.

"Yeah, in a sec," Ava says to Isabella. "I was just catching up with Sophia."

"Oh!" Isabella looks up and throws her phone into a Prada bag that's too small for her to carry books in. "Sophia! Hi! Sorry, I was barely paying attention when I walked over. You wanna come get lunch with us?"

"Sure," Sophia says, trying to gulp down the uneasy feeling bubbling up inside of her.

"Yay!" Ava links her arm with Sophia's. "Lunch with *all* my best friends."

*If Ava is friends with these people, they can't be that bad,* Sophia thinks to herself. *Besides, Isabella just invited me to hang with them for lunch. At the popular table. That's nice of her!*

Sophia walks alongside Ava and Isabella as they make their way over to the far-right annex, which everyone at Charis knows is where the most popular kids in school sit. Sophia thinks about calling an audible and quickly rerouting to literally anywhere else—but where else would she go? It's not that she doesn't have friends at school, but she's never really had a tight group the way Ava and Isabella do. Sophia is usually more of a floater with a casual friend or two in each of the lunch groups. Ava is her first real best friend.

*It's only natural that I would sit with her at lunch,* Sophia reminds herself. *Even if that means sitting at the popular table.*

Sophia takes a deep breath and slides in next to Ava at their

table. Isabella casually glides into the seat across from them.

"Where are Vivi and Manija?" Sophia asks, looking around. Vivi Jones and Manija Hajj are the two other members of Isabella and Ava's lunch group. "Don't they usually sit here too?"

"Ugh, who knows," Isabella says, rolling her eyes as she mixes dressing into her salad.

"Oh, are you guys not friends anymore?" Sophia asks, confused. Wouldn't Ava mention something as major as dropping two of her best friends? "Sorry, I didn't know!"

"No, we are," Ava says, waving to Manija and Vivi from across the room as they make their way over. "Isabella is just annoyed with them right now—she gets annoyed *super* easily."

"It's true," Isabella says with a shrug. "I do. Mani and Vivi are still our besties, though."

"Oh," Sophia says, the uneasiness bubbling up inside of her again. "Got it."

"Hey, girls," Manija says sliding in next to Ava. "Ugh, this day has already been *brutal*. Mr. Russel gave a pop quiz in math. Who gives a pop quiz on the first day of school?"

"It's seriously evil," Vivi agrees, taking a seat next to Isabella. "I would protest."

"No, you wouldn't," Isabella says. "Your mom grounds you for getting an A minus. You would get sent to military school for refusing to take a pop quiz."

"It was just hyperbole, Isabella," Ava chimes in. "Relax."

"Hyper what?" Isabella asks.

"Hyperbole," Ava repeats. "It means, like, an exaggeration. I'm practicing for the vocab portion of the high school entrance exams."

Sophia notices Manija and Vivi shoot each other looks and quietly giggle. She hopes they aren't making fun of Ava.

"So, um, how was everyone's summer?" Sophia tries to change the subject.

"Oh, Sophia!" Manija looks at her. "I didn't realize you were here. Welcome to the table."

"Um, thanks," Sophia says.

"Yeah, welcome," Vivi chimes in. "How are things with your boyfriend? Ryan, right?"

"Yeah, Ryan," Sophia says. "We aren't boyfriend and girlfriend anymore. My parents weren't really into that, so we broke up. But we actually have a couple classes together this year and it's not as awkward as I thought it would be."

"Wait, you didn't tell me that!" Ava exclaims. "I'm so glad things weren't weird."

"Yeah, I mean, they were *slightly* awkward," Sophia admits. "But I'm hoping we can just become friends as the year goes on."

"I bet you'll be able to," Ava says with a reassuring smile.

"Anyway," Manija cuts in. "Did you all see Paloma Riviera's shoes? She thinks they're cool, but they're so weird."

"I liked them!" Ava jumps to Paloma's defense. "Why do you always have to be so mean about other people's outfits?"

"Yeah," Sophia agrees. "I liked Paloma's shoes. They were different."

"I thought they looked like a rainbow barfed on her feet," Isabella says, still absently scrolling through her phone.

"*Not* nice," Ava says. "Remember, Isabella? We're working on niceness."

Sophia doesn't get it. *How is Ava friends with these girls?* She opens her mouth to say something, but then shuts it. *These are Ava's friends*, she reminds herself. *She can call them out, but I shouldn't.* Ava was so excited to have Sophia hanging with her crew. The last thing Sophia wants to do is burst her BFF's bubble. *I'll just keep to myself when I hang with them and share any not-so-great opinions with Baba or my parents,* she decides.

As she tries her best to tune out the girls' heated debate on whether or not Paloma's shoes are cool, Sophia notices a yellow flyer hanging on the bulletin board behind Isabella.

GIRLS' HIP-HOP DANCE CLASS

Do you have what it takes to be part of Charis's prestigious hip-hop dance program?

Then come audition next Friday after school at the gym!

Practices will be on Tuesdays, 3:30–4:30 p.m.

Go swans!

Sophia has never admitted this to anyone, but she's secretly dreamt of being part of the famed hip-hop dance program here at Charis. She decides to grab a flyer after lunch once she's parted ways with Ava's crew. Sophia gulps, a little intimidated by the idea of going after such a far-fetched dream. *I just won't make a big deal about this unless I make the team,* she tells herself.

The rest of the school day breezes by much more quickly than that lunch period, and before she knows it, Sophia is in the car with her mom and Alan. Sophia breathes a sigh of relief as she clicks her seatbelt and leans back into her seat.

"How was school?" her mom asks.

"Tiring," Sophia says.

"Cool!" Alan says.

As her mom drives out of the parking lot, Sophia suddenly remembers how she had cut her off at dinner last night. "What did you do today, Mom?" Sophia asks. "Did you do more stuff for your golf thing and decide on the... um, I forget. Was it orchids?"

"Yes," Alan calls out from the backseat. "She was worried they would be cliché. Don't you listen to anything?"

"Oh, forget about that, Soph," her mom says, letting out a laugh. "I want to hear all about your days. Tell me everything!"

"You go first, Alan," Sophia says, noticing a text from Lily flashing across her phone screen. "I have to respond to these texts really quick."

"Sophia, don't you want to hear about your brother's day?" her mom asks. "It was the first day of school. This is a big deal!"

"I know," Sophia says as she's clicking on her phone. "And I promise I'll listen to his day while I respond."

"It is very rude to listen to someone while you're on the phone, Sophia," her mom says, using her stern tone. "So, if it's that important to you, why don't you send your message first, then we can all listen to each other's days without any phone interference. Okay?"

"Okay," Sophia agrees, resisting the urge to roll her eyes. *Imagine what she would do if she saw how Isabella Rossi uses her phone*, Sophia thinks to herself.

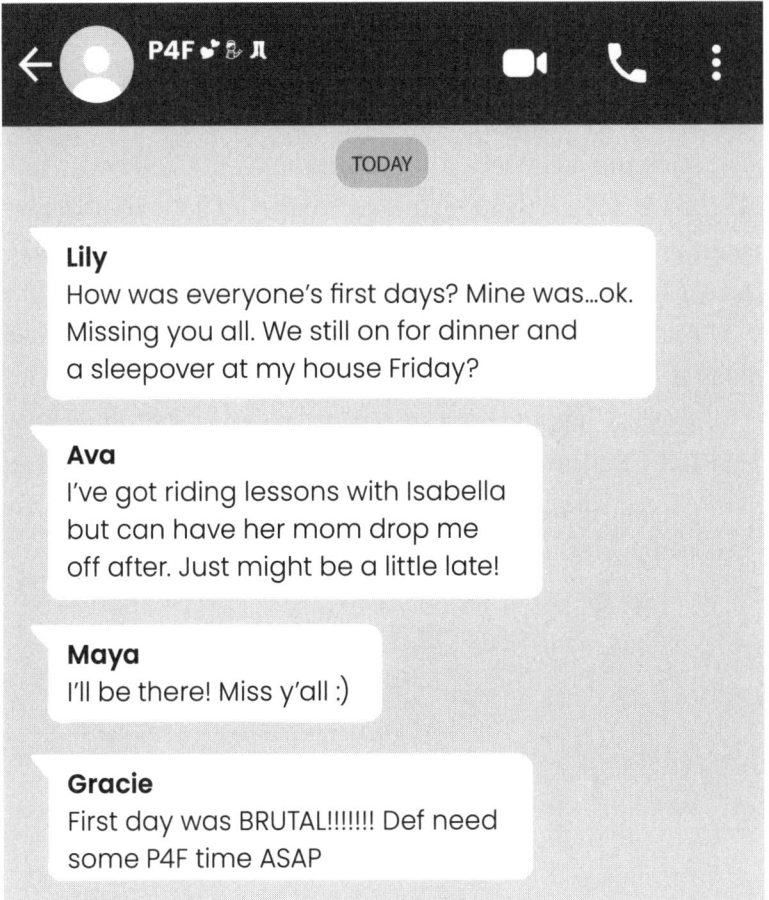

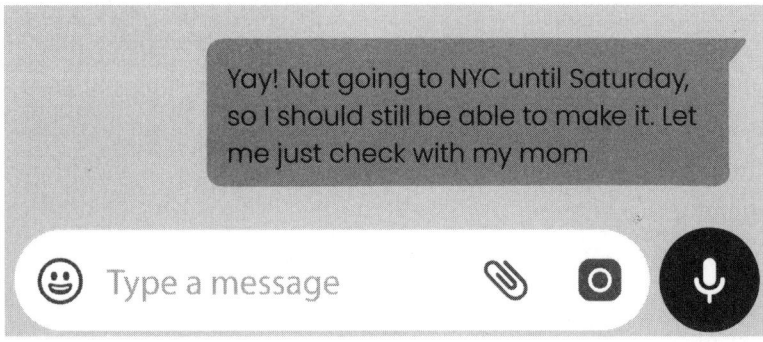

"Done?" Sophia's mom asks.

"Yup. Mom?" Sophia looks up, plopping her phone into one of the two cup holders between herself and her mom. "Do you mind if I go to Lily's on Friday for a sleepover?"

Her mom considers it for a minute. "I don't see why not. Maybe I could pick you up a little earlier on Saturday and we could grab breakfast? That way we could log in some quality time before you're at your dad's."

"Yeah, sure, that sounds fine," Sophia says, too excited about going to Lily's take in what her mom is even suggesting.

As Alan begins talking about his first day of school, Sophia's mind drifts away. She hasn't seen the P4F girls in over a week now and they have so much to catch up on. Friday can't come soon enough.

# nine

Set up in the Smiths' big library upstairs, with sleeping bags spread across the floor, the girls huddle around Sophia as she shows them on her phone the looks she found at the Met last week. As she swipes through, she gives a running commentary of what she remembers of each of the designers.

"And I thought this one was so you, Lil," Sophia says as the white wedding dress flashes across her phone screen. "So classic and cool."

"I *love* it," Lily gushes. "It sort of reminds me of the one my mom wore for her wedding. I used to stare at those photos all the time."

"I wish I could've gone to the Met! That ombre floral dress is stuck in my head like a Kacey Musgraves song," Maya says, plopping back onto the red sleeping bag she embroidered with white paisley print.

Sophia looks down at her neon-green sleeping bag, which she embellished by sewing on silver star-shaped patches. Each of the girls designed their own sleeping bags at the P4F sleeping bag decorating party Gracie hosted a few weeks ago. Gracie added a giant patent leather skull to her pink sleeping bag, while Maya put a paisley print on her red one. Ava brought a navy sleeping bag that she embroidered with tiny white satin flowers, which Sophia thinks suits her friend perfectly. Lily decorated her white sleeping bag by sewing her name in pastel-colored block letters.

Sophia rubs one of the silver stars on her sleeping bag as she thinks about the Met Gala exhibit. "I was so inspired there. We have to get back to Zoey's Closet ASAP. Did Ms. Anna say when classes will be?"

"My mama's schedule is pretty flexible, so it really just depends on what works for all of us," Gracie says. "Sophia, Saturdays are obviously out for you since you're going to New York every weekend. Anyone else have any days that they can't do?"

"Can we pick a date later?" Ava asks as she lies down. "I'm so full of challah right now. I need a minute to relax before I think about my schedule."

Lily nods. "Actually, I sort of have a sweet tooth. Do you all want to order some dessert?"

"Yes!" Maya says. "My mom was baking a Texas sheet cake for the bake sale at my parish this weekend and I've been craving something sweet ever since."

Sophia flicks a piece of lint off her avocado-print flannel pajamas and scans the room around her. Ever since their first Friday night sleepover here over the summer, it has become their tradition to gather at one of their houses for their version of a Shabbat dinner followed by a slumber party.

Sophia looks forward to it every week and especially loves it when they have it at Lily's house. Mr. Smith, a professor at University of Pennsylvania, always makes the library look so special, with twinkle lights lining the wall-to-wall bookshelves and their sleeping bags laid out in a circle atop the antique Persian rug that covers the hardwood floors.

"How about Insomnia cookies?" Sophia suggests, her eyes scanning the mesmerizing library. "My dad and I used to get them when we were in the city. They're so good."

"I've seen people ordering Insomnia on social media but have never tried it myself," Ava says, the feather trim of her silk pajamas bouncing around as she waves her hands in the air. She sits up. "Lily, do you think your dad will be okay with us eating up here? I would hate to defile this exquisite library with crumbs."

"Defile? Exquisite?" Gracie asks, one eyebrow raised, before quickly remembering. "Oh, the vocab thing. I remember from the group chat."

As the girls giggle over the fancy words Ava's been popping into their group chat all week long, Sophia can't help but remember the way Manija and Vivi laughed during lunch on Monday over the same thing. But while the P4F girls are laughing *with* Ava, it felt like Manija and Vivi were laughing *at* her.

"My dad won't mind us eating up here," Lily says. "He already texted me to let him know if we want him to pick anything up. I'll just reply now and tell him we're thinking Insomnia."

"Great," Ava says, launching into business mode. "So, what kind of cookies are we thinking? Since most of us haven't tried Insomnia yet, maybe an assortment would be best. That way we can try everything."

"Great idea," Lily says, pausing before typing up the order to her dad. "Does that work for everyone?"

"Works for me," Sophia says, her mouth already watering at the thought of a warm chocolate chip cookie. "So, while we wait for the desserts to arrive—Lil, why don't we discuss your bat mitzvah? It's coming up soon, right?"

"Soonish," Lily replies. "I haven't even started my one-on-one meetings with my rabbi yet."

"This will be my first bat mitzvah," Maya says. "I am so excited. My best friend Casey from home just had hers and her

TikToks made it seem like a blast."

"It will be my first one too," Gracie says. "What are they like?"

"In Judaism, you become an adult at thirteen, so the whole point of the bat mitzvah is to mark the transition to womanhood," Lily explains. "The event will start with a ceremony where I read from the Torah, then we'll have a party to celebrate."

"Whoa, so do you feel like a woman?" Maya asks, her eyes wide.

Lily lets out a snort. "Not at *all*. I still can't sleep without my stuffed panda."

"Ruby Rubenstein *is* a cutie," Maya says, reaching a hand over to pet the stuffed animal safely tucked into Lily's sleeping bag. "Hey, Ruby's outfit even sort of matches mine!"

Sophia lets out a laugh. Maya is right. Ruby's dressed in long, classic-looking pajamas with a light-yellow floral print. Meanwhile, Maya is dressed in pajamas similarly cut with a multicolored floral print.

"Rubes has always had a thing for fashion," Lily says, squeezing her stuffed animal tight to her chest. "You know, these little pajamas are actually one of the first things I ever sewed. My mom and I made them together—just a few months before her cancer diagnosis. I realized I had grown too tall for one of my favorite sundresses and I was sad about

79

letting it go, so my mom had the idea to repurpose the fabric into an outfit for Ruby."

"It's so cute," Ava says, her eyes visibly watering upon hearing her friend's sweet memory with her late mother. "Your mom sounds awesome—er, transcendent."

"If that means she was the best, you're right," Lily says with a soft smile. "I wish she could be around for my bat mitzvah. My Aunt Amelia is helping a lot with planning, but she just doesn't get me the way my mom did. Like, my aunt wants me to do a Candyland theme for the party. I barely even eat candy!"

"So, why don't we help you think of a new theme?" Ava suggests. "One you're actually excited about?"

"Yes!" Gracie says. "This sounds so fun. Let's brainstorm theme ideas!"

"Okay," Lily agrees. "But I have to warn you guys, coming up with a theme idea has been way more difficult than I expected it to be."

"That's because you've been trying to do it without us," Ava says matter-of-factly. "With all five of our brains combined, we'll come up with a theme in no time."

"Okay, so, we know you love fashion," Gracie begins. "Ooh! What if everyone had to make their own outfits? It would be like the fashion show 2.0."

"Well, *I* would obviously love that," Lily says. "But not everyone likes sewing like we do—or even knows how."

Gracie frowns. "True... but that doesn't mean we have to totally ditch the fashion theme. What if we did something else? Like... ooh! What if we did our favorite looks in fashion history? I already know what I would wear. That black outfit with the rubies on the sleeves that Willow Smith wore to the Vanity Fair Oscar party."

"I would go for that white taffeta gown I showed you girls from the Met Gala," Sophia says, remembering the moment she shared with her dad over the dress. "But doesn't that go back to Lily's main issue? Not everyone is as into fashion as we are. What if people don't have favorite looks they can easily come up with?"

"All right, how about we get inspiration from a movie instead?" Ava suggests. "Like, a movie that has an obvious fashion theme?"

"That's a great idea," Maya says, nodding enthusiastically. "That way people can just watch the movie and pick an outfit without thinking too much about it."

"Yep," Ava says. "And! It gives you a more cohesive theme to go off of for, like, decorating the venue and stuff."

"I think you might be on to something," Lily says, her lips curling up in excitement. "A movie would be perfect!"

"Now there's just one thing left to decide," Sophia says. "Lil, what's your favorite fashion movie?"

"Easy," Lily says. "*Clueless*. I've seen it at least a hundred times. When my mom was sick, we would snuggle in bed and watch it together. It's kind of like one of my only good memories from that time. Plus, it's the first movie we all watched together."

"*Clueless* is kind of like this house," Maya says with a smile. "It's magic. My mom always says she thinks that movie is what sparked my love of fashion."

"It sparked mine too," Sophia nods. "Honestly, I was kind of hoping you would pick *Clueless* when I asked, Lil. It's pretty much the only PG-13 my mom lets me watch and by far my favorite movie ever."

"I can't wait to be Dionne!" Ava exclaims. "Decision made!"

"Cookie delivery!" Lily's dad announces as he walks in with a box of cookies along with some paper plates and napkins. "Everything going well up here?"

"Better than that," Lily says, helping herself to a chocolate chip cookie as soon as her dad places the boxes down on the floor by their sleeping bags. "I think we thought of a theme for my bat mitzvah!"

"It's going to be *Clueless*," Gracie excitedly chimes in. "The only thing we have left to do is pick a new day for our P4F classes."

Ava takes a large bite of a white-frosted cookie and sighs happily. "Now that I have some sugar in my system, I am all

in to talk scheduling."

"I'll let you girls get to it then," Mr. Smith says, making his way out of the library. "Lily, just make sure not to double-book with your cantor's class or soccer."

"I will," Lily responds. "Thanks for the cookies, Dad."

"Thank you, Mr. Smith!" the rest of the girls echo after her as they dig into the cookies.

"So," Maya says after Lily's dad leaves, "Saturdays are out. But how about Sundays? That way it won't interfere with any of our extracurriculars. I have church in the morning but could meet up for class right after."

"I might have soccer games on weekends," Lily says, nervously biting her nail. "And I would hate to have to miss some classes for that."

"Weekends are not the best for me either," Sophia adds. "I'll be going back and forth to my dad's most weekends, so I'm not really sure how I would make it work."

"And Fridays we already have our sleepover tradition," Ava adds. "I have something pretty much every day, but they mostly end around four or four-thirty. So, I could do any day of the week if we agree to do an evening, closer to five. Maybe we could do class for an hour then grab dinner together?"

"I could talk to my mama and see if she would let us eat dinner during class," Gracie says. "I bet she would be!"

"That would be amazing!" Maya says. "But what day? I have Bible study on Wednesdays and it can go pretty late."

"I have my cantor's class on Tuesdays and I have no idea how late it will go," Lily notes. "Then there's soccer on Wednesdays and Fridays until five."

"How about Monday?" Sophia asks. It's usually her least

favorite day of the week, but having P4F classes would make it better. "Mondays are so brutal, and this could be a fun way to make them less painful."

"It totally would be," Ava thinks aloud. "Buuuut there's pretty much no way my parents would let me kick off the school week with a fashion class."

The girls finally agree Thursday nights would be it. *Getting back in the studio is going to be epic, no matter what the day,* Sophia thinks happily as she munches on her cookie.

# ten

As everyone is still soundly asleep in the library, Sophia quietly walks down the stairs and opens the front door. Her mom is so intent on skipping the traffic to New York that she and Alan are here at Lily's at six in the morning to pick Sophia up.

"Wow, honey, this is one heavy bag," Sophia's mom says as she helps her daughter stuff her weekend bag into the car. "How much did you pack in here?"

"I had to pack for Lily's *and* for a weekend in the city with Dad," Sophia explains. "That's a lot of outfits!"

"I don't get it," Alan says with a yawn, looking her up and down from where he's sitting in the backseat. "Why can't you just wear what you're wearing now today *and* tomorrow?"

Sophia looks down at the boyfriend jeans she's thrown on with some Air Force 1s. On top, she's wearing a Ralph Lauren men's pinstripe button-down open over a white bodysuit. "I mean, I *can*, but I want to build a wardrobe at Dad's so I don't have to keep bringing stuff back and forth. Everything I packed is proper city attire that's going to stay in New York."

"I hope you managed to squeeze some textbooks in there, Soph," her mom says. "I don't want these trips to leave you behind on your schoolwork. Your father and I both agree that school should always come first."

"I did," Sophia mumbles, a knot forming in her stomach as she thinks of all the schoolwork she hasn't finished yet. "Can I go say bye to my friends before we leave? Maybe they'll be awake now."

"Sure, hon," her mom says. "Just be quick! We don't want to get stuck in that Holland Tunnel traffic again."

Sophia quietly makes her way up the stairs into the library and sees Ava and Gracie quietly whispering to each other from their sleeping bags. *They're up!* Sophia thinks.

"There you are," Ava whispers as Sophia tiptoes over to them. "We were just wondering where you went."

"My mom came to pick me up super early," Sophia whispers back. "I just wanted to come back here and say bye in case any of you were up."

"Bye, Soph," Gracie says, reaching her arms around her for a hug. "Have fun in New York! Don't forget to take pictures for me if you see any cool punk clothes."

"Yeah, we're going to miss you at breakfast," Ava adds, wrapping her arms around her two friends. "Lily said her dad's making pancakes."

"Shoot, his pancakes are so good," Sophia sighs. "Next time, I guess. I'll see you at school on Monday, Aves. Gracie, see you on Thursday for P4F. Tell the others bye for me when they wake up."

"Don't forget to keep us posted on all the fun things you

do this weekend!" Ava says as Sophia stands to leave. "No way you can outdo those *superb* Met pics, but at least try."

"I will," Sophia says. She gives one last wave before quietly closing the library door behind her.

*This is so hard*, she thinks to herself as she makes her way back to her mom's car. *When I leave New York, all I can think about is how much I miss the city. And when I leave Lower Merion, all I can think about is how much I miss home.*

"You okay, sweetie?" her mom asks, looking over at her from the driver's seat. "You seem kind of down."

"Yeah, I'm fine," Sophia says. "Just going to miss my friends, you know?"

"Well, you don't have to go to New York," her mom suggests.

"Just stay here! Spend a weekend with your girls and you can be in New York next week..."

"No," Sophia cuts her mom off a little more sharply than she means to. "I *want* to go to New York. I miss the city and I miss Dad. And Baba. And Lyla. I just... wish everybody could be there."

"Yeah," Alan chimes in from the backseat. "Theo and Marcus have a chess tournament today in Lower Merion, but I have to miss it to go to the city. I wish the chess tournament could be *there* instead."

"I'm sorry, kids," their mom sighs. "I wish there was an easier way to do this. But hey, we've still got a nice breakfast ahead of us, right?"

"Oh, um, about that... Mom, would you mind if we just went straight to Dad's?" Sophia asks, her voice coming out a bit shaky. "I just... I really miss him. And I feel like I only get a certain amount of hours with him on these weekends, so I don't want to waste..."

"...your time with me," her mom finishes her sentence. "I get it."

"No, 'waste' isn't the right word," Sophia says quickly. "Just... you know what I mean. I'm with you all the time! I only get a couple days to be with Dad. Don't you want to go see your New York friends anyway?"

"Don't worry about it, Soph," her mom says, a fake smile plastered across her face. "It's fine! You're right. I see you kids all the time. Probably best to let your dad enjoy his time with you."

Alan frowns. "I'll get breakfast with you if you want, Mom."

"It's okay, sweetie," their mom replies, her eyes set on the road ahead. "You two just enjoy being with your dad."

The car falls into awkward silence while Sophia looks out the window, feeling guilty. When they finally get to their dad's house, Sophia's mom parks the car by the curb but doesn't turn off the engine.

"I'll just wait here to make sure you kids get in okay," she says with a smile. "I should get going. Gigi wants me to meet her at the club this afternoon to run through the charity golf tournament."

"And Gigi hates tardiness," Sophia says. "All right. Well, I guess it's time to say bye?"

"Bye, sweetie," her mom says, kissing her cheek so hard that it leaves an imprint of her nude-pink lipstick. "Be good, okay?"

Alan shouts as he rushes over to buzz her dad's door. "See you tomorrow!"

"See you, honey!" her mom shouts back. "Love you both to the moon!"

As soon as they hear the sound of their dad's voice over the intercom and he buzzes them in, Sophia and Alan wave as their mom drives off.

"I think we should have gotten breakfast with her," Alan says to Sophia as they get into the elevator. "She seemed sad."

"She'll get over it," Sophia says with a halfhearted shrug. "We get five whole days of the week with her and only twenty-four hours this week with Dad! She has to understand that."

Before Alan can respond, the elevator doors open to their dad's living room.

"There are my favorite kids!" he says as both Sophia and Alan run into his arms.

"It feels so good to be back," Sophia says, squeezing him tight. "I couldn't stop thinking about the city the whole time I was home."

"And now you're back!" Her dad gives her a quick kiss on the head before he gets back up. "I have a feeling you're both going to like what I have in store for today."

Sophia looks up at her dad eagerly and wonders what he has in mind. Shopping? Another museum? *Maybe we'll go to Domino Park*, she thinks. *That used to be our favorite place to hang out.*

"Alan, I heard from your mom that you were a little bummed about missing your friends' chess tournament," her dad says. "So, I was thinking maybe you and I could go to Battery Park and have a chess tournament of our own! A few hours of uninterrupted father-son chess."

"Awesome!" Alan yells, jumping up and down for joy. "I'll go throw my stuff in my room and then we can go!"

"What about me?" Sophia asks quietly, resisting the urge to cry as Alan runs excitedly into his room. "You guys are just going to ditch me all day?"

"That is not it at all," a voice interrupts. Sophia's eyes widen in surprise as she sees Baba making her over from the kitchen. "I told these silly boys to give us the apartment for the next few hours so *we* could spend some time together. We can make Butajiru and paint your duvet cover."

"Baba!" Sophia hugs her grandmother, her mood immediately brightening. Cooking is what she and Baba like to do when they *really* want to catch up. It has been way too long since Sophia spent time with her Baba, just the two of them. She didn't even realize how much she misses it until just now.

After Alan and her dad leave, Sophia and Baba immediately get to work. Sophia ties on an apron and washes her hands as Baba pulls out the ingredients they need.

"So, Sophia, tell your Baba," Baba says once they're sitting alongside her dad's kitchen island peeling carrots for the soup. "How are *you* doing?"

Sophia thinks for a minute. Things have been moving so quickly that she hasn't really had a minute to process how she's feeling.

"I... I'm not really sure, Baba," Sophia admits. "It's hard not having Dad in Lower Merion. But at the same time, I love coming back to the city. Everything just feels so right here."

"You have always been a little city girl," Baba says, flashing Sophia a knowing smile. "How was the first day of school? Did you wear your new backpack?"

"Yes, I wore the backpack and I *loved* it," she says. "Ava is practicing her vocab for the high school entrance tests and she said I looked 'arresting yet perennial.' I looked those up and it pretty much means I nailed it."

"That is nice you have Ava at school," Baba says. "Having a best friend is a special gift."

"I know," Sophia says. She sets down her peeler and begins to chop the carrots in thin slices. "I also had lunch with her and her friends... but they aren't really my favorite people. They're just sort of mean to each other. Not like Ava at all. I don't get what she sees in them."

"I'm sure Ava has her reasons for liking them," Baba says, setting her chopped carrots in a bowl and carefully slicing the pork butt. "Do you have anyone else you can hang out with at school?"

"Remember Ryan?" Sophia asks, her voice lowering to a whisper even though her dad and Alan have been gone for a while now.

"Of course I do," Baba responds, one eyebrow raised.

"Okay, so I broke up with him when Mom and Dad told me to," Sophia recounts. "I didn't even miss him that much once we split, to be honest. But guess who sits next to me in homeroom this year?"

"Ryan?"

"Yes!" Sophia exclaims. "Seeing him sort of just... brought some of those old feelings back."

"Too soon for boys, Sophi-chan," Baba says gently, using Sophia's nickname. "Just be patient."

"I know, but he's really nice," Sophia groans as she moves on to peeling the gobo. "We get along so well."

"So maybe he can be a good friend," Baba suggests. "The classroom is a great place to form a new friendship."

"Yeah, I hope he wants to be my friend," Sophia says. "Right now I would say we're friend-*ly* but not quite *friends*, you know?"

"I know you'll get there eventually," Baba says, slicing the last of the pork butt. "You have a good head on your shoulders, Sophia."

"Thanks, Baba," Sophia says. "I'm trying my best... but I hate being away from you and Dad. And when I'm here, I hate being away from my life at home. I wish this could all be easier."

"Adjustments like this take time," Baba says, heating the large ceramic pot with oil. "You'll get used to this new system. I promise."

*I sure hope so*, Sophia thinks to herself. She knows Baba is probably right. Baba is pretty much always right. There's a reason Sophia trusts her so much. Maybe this really will eventually all start to feel okay. But, she wonders, *how am I supposed to manage all these uneasy feelings until then?*

On Sunday afternoon after getting back home, Sophia finally sits down and looks at the giant pile of books sitting atop her desk. She doesn't even know where to begin. Mom was right, she thinks to herself. *I should have been doing some homework at Dad's.*

She quickly pulls out her phone and FaceTimes Ava. She knows she should just dive into all this work, but sometimes a little solidarity is nice. The phone rings once, before Ava declines the call.

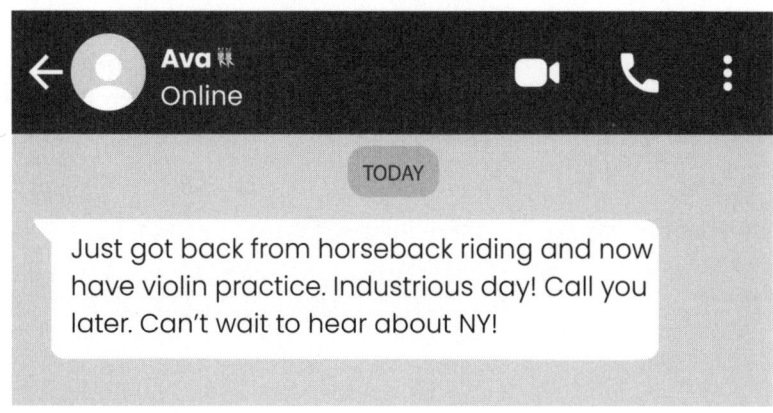

Sophia sighs. Ava probably finished all of Monday's homework on Friday. Even though she would probably never let her homework pile up the way Sophia does, Sophia knows Ava gets just as stressed about schoolwork as she does, if not more. Sophia could really use a conversation with someone who gets how overwhelming Charis can be.

Then she remembers Ryan. *If we're going to make the transition from friendly to real friends, someone has to make the first move. Right?* she thinks to herself.

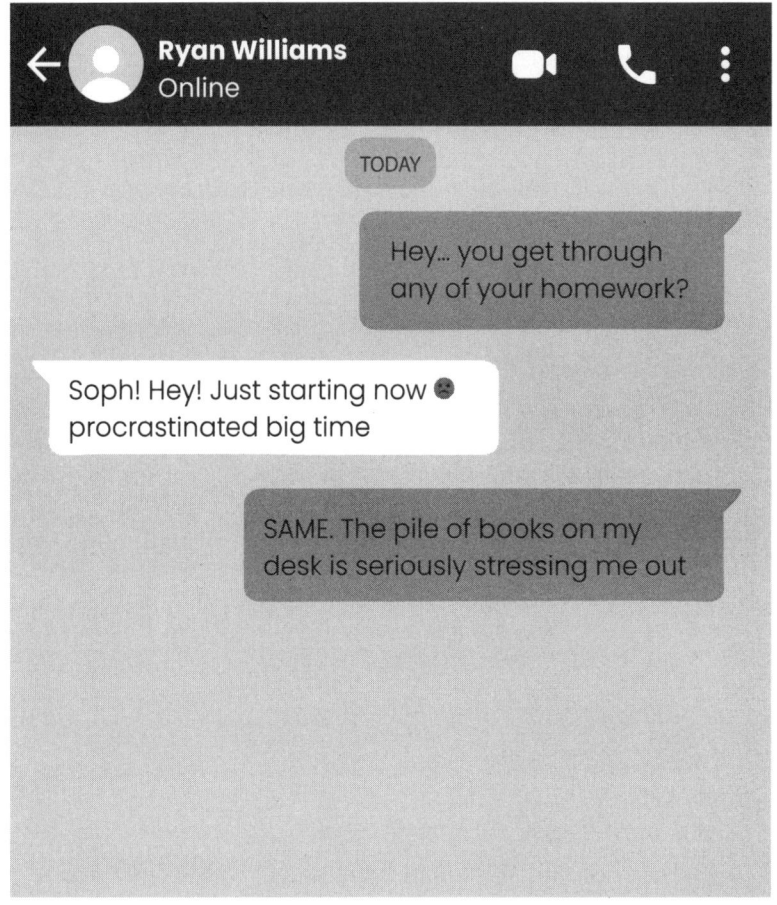

Oh man. That is a lot. But mine might be worse

Yikes. What do you have this week?

3 tests. 2 essays. And an art project. The essay and the test are tomorrow, so cramming right now. HBU?

I'm too scared to look at my planner. But I know I have quiz and an essay tomorrow. Probably a sign that I should stop texting and get to work...

Maybe we can quiz each other in homeroom to prep?

You bet

Hey Soph?

What's up?

It's cool that we're talking again

Agreed.

 Type a message

Sophia smiles as she plugs her phone into the charger on her nightstand. She was so excited to have a boyfriend when Ryan asked her out over the summer. But being his friend feels more comfortable. Her parents were right—she's not ready for boyfriends just yet. For now, her focus is best spent on the mountain of books piled up on her desk.

"Soph," her mom says, knocking on the door once before letting herself in. "How's the homework coming along?"

"Not super well," Sophia admits. "It feels like so much."

"What do you have going on?" her mom asks. "Maybe I can help."

Sophia pulls her planner out of the mound of books and looks at what she has coming up for the week ahead. "I have a *lot*," Sophia says, her heart speeding up as she takes in the amount of blue ink scribbled on the pages. "I have a book report on *Stargirl*, plus I have to make a collage to describe visually how it made me feel due tomorrow."

"Have you read it yet?" her mom asks. "Because that's the hard part."

"Yeah, I finished it on Thursday," Sophia says, pulling the book out of her pile. "And look! I even put sticky notes on the pages I want to quote."

Her mom gives her a proud grin. "You know I've been trying to get you to do that forever."

"I know," Sophia says. "I thought you would be happy. It makes my life way easier anyway."

"So, is it just the book report and the collage?" her mom asks. "I think we could easily knock those out today."

"Not really," Sophia says, looking back down at her planner. "I also have a math quiz on ratios tomorrow. Then

I've got a *lot* going on the rest of the week. Like, I have an essay on the Byzantine Empire due Wednesday for history. I also have a biology test that day, then I have an oral Spanish exam on Thursday."

"I know you don't like when I say I told you so," her mom begins. Sophia can already sense where she's going with this. "But I do think you would be a lot less stressed on Sundays if you did some schoolwork with your dad on Saturdays. Or even on Fridays before your sleepover. It's all about time management, Soph."

"I know, I know, I know," Sophia groans. "You're right. But your rightness doesn't help me with how much I have to do right now!"

"Is that everything?" her mom asks. "The English paper and collage, plus the math quiz tomorrow. Then the history paper, the biology test, and the oral Spanish exam later this week?"

"Almost," Sophia says, remembering the yellow slip of paper she pulled off the bulletin board on Monday. "There's one more thing I was sort of hoping to do this week. It's an after-school activity."

She still hasn't told anyone about hip-hop. But if she really wants to make this happen, then telling her mom is the first step.

"What is it?" her mom asks. "I'm always happy to sign you up for more extracurriculars. They look excellent on high school applications."

Sophia shuffles through everything on her desk and finds the crumpled piece of paper tucked into her history textbook.

"I know it's kind of random," Sophia says, handing the

flyer over to her mom. "But I saw the hip-hop girls perform last year at an assembly and they were really good. They meet on Tuesdays, which is perfect because we just decided P4F will be on Thursdays, so it doesn't conflict with that."

"Sophia, this is *wonderful*," her mom bursts. "Charis is known for their dance program. If you are interested in dance, there is no better place to learn. You know, I was a dancer in Charis back when I was there."

"I know," Sophia says, remembering the many pictures Gigi showed Sophia of her mom dancing at various recitals in baby-blue leotards back when she was a student at Charis. "Actually, that was mainly what I wanted to talk to you about. Since you know how to dance, do you think you could help me come up with a routine to perform at the audition? I'm kind of nervous, since I haven't really ever done anything like this before."

Sophia watches as her mom's face brightens like someone just lit a lightbulb inside of it.

"Oh, honey, I would *love* to help you!" her mom nearly shouts, giving her daughter a tight squeeze. "We are going to make the best darn routine Charis has ever seen!"

"I'll settle for decent," Sophia says with a giggle, wiggling herself loose from her mom's tight grip. "As long as it's good enough to get me in."

"It will be better than 'good enough' to get you in," her mom says with a smile. "Your name may be Sophia Ito, but you have Beck blood in your DNA, and us Becks know how to dance."

"Do you know how to do hip-hop, though?" Sophia asks. "In Gigi's pictures it seemed like you were doing ballet."

"No, I never did hip-hop," her mom admits. "I was mostly focused on jazz and ballet. But at the end of the day, dance is dance. I think I can show you the basics and we can come up with something great."

"Cool!" Sophia opens her laptop and begins typing. "Maybe we can find some hip-hop videos on YouTube for inspiration. I saw some old Paula Abdul videos with Dad and Baba earlier this summer—she was *so* good."

"First, do your homework, missy," her mom says, reaching over Sophia to exit out of YouTube. "Then I promise we can do a hip-hop video marathon for inspiration."

"Fiiiiiiine," Sophia groans. "See you in four hundred hours."

"Oh, don't be dramatic," her mom laughs. "You'll be done in no time. Then we can get to work on the routine! I love the Paula Abdul inspiration idea. She was a dancing legend."

"Maybe you can watch some videos while I do my homework," Sophia suggests. "That way, by the time I'm done, you'll have some ideas."

"No, that will take the fun out of it," her mom says, making her way to the door. "This has to be your routine, filled with moves *you* like. I'm just here to help."

"I guess that makes sense." Sophia says, already envisioning the different sorts of moves she can put together. "Thanks, Mom."

"Any time, sweetie," her mom says, making her way toward the door. "Hey, now that you're trying my hobbies out, maybe you'll finally give horseback riding a chance."

Sophia just gives her mom a strange look. *Yeah, that is so not happening*, she thinks.

101

"At least I tried," her mom says with a shrug, before shutting the door.

Before Sophia can get started on her English essay, her computer screen lights up with a call from Ava.

"Aves!" Sophia says as she answers. "Guess what."

"What?" Ava asks. "Don't tell me you got another cool backpack in the city. This sad suburban girl can officially no longer keep up."

"There's no new backpack," Sophia says. "Remember last year there was that one school assembly where the students danced hip-hop?"

"Yes," Ava says. "Wait. Are you going to try out?"

"Yes!" Sophia says. "I just talked to my mom about it—she used to dance at Charis, so she was super into it. I think she's even going to help me prepare for the audition."

"How *marvelous!*" Ava says. "You're going to be a *consummate* dancer, I can already tell. I always wanted to try hip-hop at Charis too. But I don't think my parents would ever go for it. It's hard enough getting them on board with P4F and horseback riding."

"Ugh, don't even say the H word," Sophia sighs. "My mom and I were fully bonding over the hip-hop stuff and she just *had* to make another plea for me to try horseback riding. When are she and Gigi just going to accept that horses are not my thing and never will be?"

"Parents can never understand why you don't love all the same things they do," Ava says. "It's like when my dad gets annoyed that I don't want to play backgammon with him. It's boring!"

Sophia lets out a laugh. "At least I'm not the only one dealing with this stuff," she says. Her eyes catch on her planner and she sighs. "Anyway, I should go. I have a literal mountain of homework to get through before my mom will let me start practicing for auditions."

"Yeah, I should get back to homework also," Ava agrees. "See you tomorrow!"

Sophia sets her online status to *Do Not Disturb*, opens a blank document on her screen, and gets to work. *The sooner I finish this, the sooner I get to come up with my audition,* she thinks, her toe tapping to the beat of the music playing in her head.

# twelve

"You good to try it solo this time?" Sophia's mom asks, wiping the bead of sweat off her forehead as the clean version of Jack Harlow and Lil Nas X's "Industry Baby" ends for what must be the hundredth time this week. "I think you've got the whole routine down."

"You think?" Sophia asks, nervously biting her lower lip. "I'm so used to doing it with you."

"Well, that's why you need to practice it *without* me," her mom says. "I won't be there with you at tryouts."

Her mom is right. They have been practicing this routine nonstop since they finalized it on Monday after school. But if Sophia really wants to nail tryouts tomorrow, she has to be able to do it without her mom dancing by her side.

"You'll be great, honey," her mom says, looking down at her leather Hermés Apple watch. "Come on, we've got about fifteen minutes before you have to get changed and head to P4F. If you start now, we could get four solo practice rounds in."

Sophia takes a deep breath. "Okay, I'll try it."

Her mom starts the song back again and Sophia launches into her routine. After so many repetitions, she's pleasantly surprised by how natural the moves are flowing out of her body without having her mom dance beside her. "Go, Sophia!" her mom cheers.

They practice and lose track of time until Sophia's mom looks down at her watch and gasps. By the time Sophia finally makes it to P4F class, she's ten minutes late.

"Sophia!" Gracie's mom and owner of Zoey's Closet says as Sophia rushes through the entrance of the newly renovated store. "It's so great to see you!"

"Hi, Ms. Anna," Sophia says, giving her a hug. "I'm sorry I'm late. I have tryouts for my school's hip-hop dance program tomorrow and I guess I got a little carried away."

"That's okay," Ms. Anna says. "Hip-hop sounds fun! I had no idea you were a dancer, although you did have some great moves at the fashion show."

"Thanks," Sophia says, blushing as she remembers strutting her way down the catwalk at their charity fashion show this summer. Sophia takes a long look around Zoey's Closet. "Wow, this place looks great!"

Last time she was in Zoey's Closet, the store was flooded with water that went up to Sophia's ankles. Now, thanks to the money Sophia and her P4F friends raised at their charity show over the summer, Ms. Anna was able to rebuild the entire studio. The sparkly pink linoleum floor is glistening more brightly than ever, bringing out the colors of all the fabrics and cloths hanging around the room. She also installed new fuzzy white benches underneath the street-facing windows.

"Welcome to the new studio! I call this the inspiration station," Ms. Anna says, lifting the seat up off one of the benches to reveal dozens of fashion magazines tucked inside. "I know you girls mostly get inspired online these days, but there's nothing like a good fashion magazine to get the creativity flowing sometimes."

"Ms. Anna, this is so cool," Sophia says, her eyes darting over to the wall covered with rolls and rolls of the most fun fabrics she's ever seen. "I love it even more than before."

In the center of the room is a large, round white table where all her friends are currently seated on chrome stools with white fuzzy cushions as seats. Each of them has a sewing machine placed in front of her, and Sophia can see Ms. Anna has taken the time to write each girl's name on her own sewing machine in a sparkly pink puff paint that matches the floors.

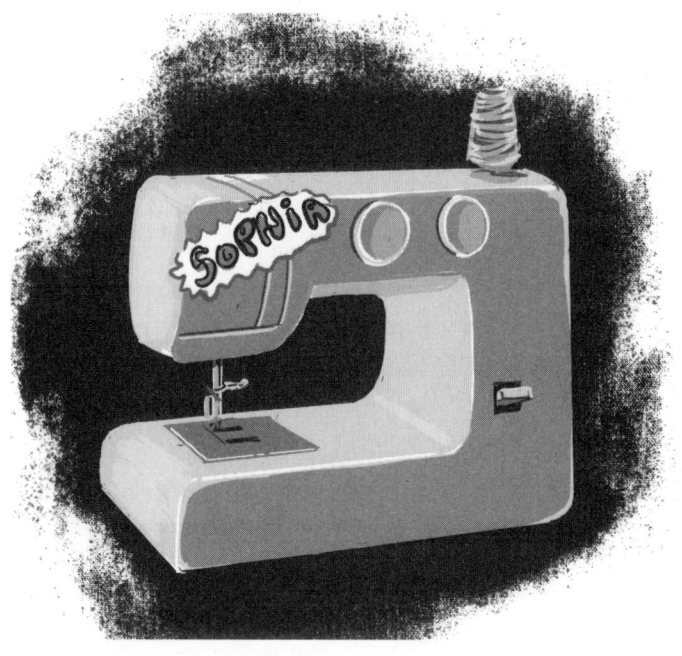

"Soph's here!" Gracie announces as Sophia makes her way over to join her friends at the table. She waves as everyone turns and shouts her name together in unison.

"Oh my gosh," Sophia says, taking a seat atop the empty chrome stool next to Ava. "I can't get over how amazing this place looks. You would never know there was even a flood!"

"I know, right?" Gracie says. "And don't you love these fun stools?"

"Yes!" Sophia exclaims. "So modern and cool."

"But I'm glad you kept the sparkly floors, Ms. Anna," Lily says. "They feel like a special part of the old Zoey's Closet."

"Well, Zoey's Closet was named after my mother," Ms. Anna says. "And the woman loved these sparkly floors. She didn't get to spend much time here in the store before she passed, but the few times she did come she would always rave about the flooring. I had to keep it in her honor."

Ava eagerly waves a swatch of fabric. "Can we tell Sophia what we're making now? I'm sorry, I'm just too exuberant to suppress it any longer."

"Of course! So, Sophia," Ms. Anna explains, "the girls and I were just brainstorming about what to create today and Ava had a great idea. We think you're going to love it."

"Can you all just tell me already?" Sophia asks. "The anticipation is killing me!"

"We're going to make our own iPad covers!" Maya blurts out. "Like, for school!"

Sophia thinks about the gray cover with the Charis logo stitched onto it that's currently adorning her school iPad. Every time she sees it, she thinks about getting a new one or making her own. "I love it!" she says immediately.

"Everyone uses iPads at school," Ava explains. "And no one likes a cracked screen."

"Plus, the Charis Academy iPad covers are so boring," Sophia laments, her eyes already scanning the different swatches of fabric Ms. Anna has spread across the center of the table for inspiration. "This is such a cool idea. I can't wait to create a cover that actually feels like *me*."

"Exactly!" Ava smiles. "I knew you would get it."

"I mean, you *know* I am always down to spice up our dress code, even if it's for our tablets and not ourselves in this case," Sophia says. "Count me fully in."

"I don't even have an iPad cover," Lily says. "I always just throw my iPad right into my backpack. It's only been a week of school and I've already gotten so many scratches on the screen."

"I do have a cover," Maya says, "but it's from my dad's church and it just gets me more attention than I have already been getting for being related to him."

"I have a funky zebra print cover I got with my moms at Target before school," Gracie shares. "It works, but it's just not quite punk enough for my liking."

"Then it's decided," Ms. Anna says happily. "Now as you can see, I have all these small swatches of upcycled fabric in the center of the table along with a sample iPad that I believe should be the same size as all of yours. I was thinking we could patch together our own cases on the sewing machines using our favorite swatches. Here, let me show you girls how."

Sophia watches as Ms. Anna picks up a swatch of bright orange cotton and a swatch of dark navy denim. She carefully lines them up next to each other and pins them together so that they stay put.

"Once you've got the pieces of fabric aligned, it's time to sew them together on the machine," Ms. Anna says. "What I would recommend doing is having a test swatch to make sure the stitch settings you pick work for the types of fabric you choose. So, for example, if your fabric comes out a little wrinkled, you might want to adjust the settings to make your stitching a little looser."

"Got it," Ava says, jotting everything down in her notebook. "Do you have any tips for what kind of stitch or thread would be best?"

"In this case, you have a chance to get really creative," Ms. Anna says. "You could go with a bold stitch in a bright color to add to your design, or go with something simple to

let the fabric speak for itself. You'll also want to take the type of fabric into account. For example, I have denim here and a longer stitch typically looks better on denim."

"What if I want to go with silk?" Lily asks. "What's the best stitch there?"

"I would keep it shorter for silk," Ms. Anna says, getting up from her seat. "Here, one moment. Let me grab something that I think will help you."

When she returns, Ms. Anna comes with a laminated piece of paper featuring handwritten instructions on which stitch length is best for each fabric.

"My mother wrote this up for me when I was learning to sew as a little girl," Ms. Anna says. "It's one of my prized possessions. You girls can keep it as your guide when you're figuring out which stitching to use for this."

"How special," Lily says, gazing down at the paper. "Thanks, Ms. Anna."

"Of course," Ms. Anna says, her warm smile flashing down the girls. "Now, a little bird told me we might want dinner after class. So, excuse me while I go step into the back and order us some pizza. Just holler if you have any questions."

As Ms. Anna leaves, Maya puts a new spool of thread into her sewing machine and looks over the fabrics. "Soph, Ava was just telling us how stressful this year has been at Charis. Is your schedule as packed as hers?"

"I don't think *anybody* has a schedule as packed as Ava's," Sophia says with a laugh. "But so far it hasn't been easy."

"I'm *fraught* with stress," Ava groans as she grabs a beige piece of fabric spotted with black dots. "There aren't enough hours in the day. I have so many extracurriculars, and homework is more intense than ever. I can't even enjoy conversations because I'm stressing about working in vocab words whenever I can!"

Sophia nods. "I second the homework part. I left everything until Sunday this past weekend, and I wound up staying up until midnight working! My mom and I were going to start coming up with my hip-hop routine and we had to push it off until early Monday morning."

"Hip-hop?" Lily asks. "I didn't know you danced, Sophia! Some of my friends back in New York did hip-hop and I always thought it was so fun going to see their recitals."

Gracie takes a patch of magenta pleather fabric and places it on top of a black-and-white checkered patch. "Doesn't Charis have like a really, really good dance program?" she asks as she lines the two swatches up next to each other. "A girl from our neighborhood danced there and now she's on Broadway!"

"It's number one in the country," Ava says. "If Sophia makes it, you all have to come with me to cheer her on at her shows."

"Ava, would you ever want to do dance?" Maya asks, sifting through the swatches until she settles on a blue paisley patch. "It would be so fun if you both got to do it together!"

"I wish," Ava sighs. "I just don't have room for any more extracurriculars this year. Maybe next year? I could swap one of my high school entrance prep courses for hip-hop."

Sophia envisions herself and her bestie rocking it on the dance floor together. "Yes! Please do it next year. We would have so much fun."

"Wait, sorry for changing the subject. But this just popped in my head and I have to ask before it pops back out," Gracie interjects. "Sophia, have you seen Ryan at school?"

"They have *two* classes together," Ava blurts out. "Homeroom *and* English! Can you believe it?"

"Yep," Sophia says. "He was literally the first person I saw on my first day of school. Honestly, it was kind of a shock seeing him at first... but things haven't been as weird as I thought they'd be. If anything, I think we're sort of becoming friends? I really like hanging out with him without all that boyfriend pressure."

"That sounds great," Lily says. She picks up scissors and begins to cut mint green and white swatches into carefully measured stripes. "You said things felt a little awkward after you had to break up with him."

"Yeah, but we're totally cool now," Sophia says, thinking of the texts they've exchanged. "Anyway, what about you, Gracie? Have you seen Ali at all?"

Just the mention of her crush's name has Gracie's face as pink as her hair.

"I see him *everywhere*," Gracie says. "We have three classes together and yesterday we even walked home from school together."

"I'm still not really into boys," Lily admits. "But even I can tell this is a big update!"

Ava nods. "Seriously. You went from secretly crushing on him to hanging all the time in a matter of weeks! What happened?"

"Well, we both had math last period and, you know, he lives so close to me," Gracie says, her smile growing increasingly wide as she continues. "So, I just suggested we walk home together and he said sure."

Sophia looks at how happy her friend is and grins. "Sounds like this year is going way better than you were expecting it to," she says, remembering how her friend was dreading another friendless year at school.

"Yeah, and it's not even about my crush on him," Gracie says. "It's just nice having someone I'm actually looking forward to seeing at school. The fact that I have a crush on him is just a fun bonus."

Maya grins at her. "My friends were my favorite part of going to school back home in Texas too."

"How's the friend situation at your new school?" Sophia asks Maya. "Have you met anyone?"

"Honestly? It hasn't been great," Maya sighs. "The whole point of going to the Friends school was so I can get to know people who don't already know me as 'Pastor Alvarez's daughter,' but I feel like I'm just as much in the spotlight as I was at my old school."

"Do lots of his parishioners go to your school?" Lily asks.

Maya nods. "Almost everyone in my class belongs to my church. So every time someone talks to me, I can't tell whether they want to be friends with me because they like me, or because of my parents."

"I bet they want to be friends with you for *you*," Ava says as she examines different options for zippers. "I mean, you're the best—er, you're *supreme*. Why would they not want to be your friend?"

"Yeah," Gracie says, attaching the neon-pink zipper to her case. "Who cares if they know who your parents are? The way I see it, people should be kissing up to your parents because *they* get to have Maya Alvarez as a daughter."

"Thanks," Maya says with a giggle. "That means a lot. I'm sure I'll find my crew there. But for now, at least I have you all."

"Starting a new school hasn't been the easiest for me either," Lily says in her quiet voice. "I think I clicked with you all so well that I sort of forgot how tricky making new friends can be. It's hard to open up sometimes... But I've met a few girls through soccer who I really like hanging with."

"Are you going to invite them to your bat mitzvah?" Maya asks.

"Maybe. I haven't really thought about the bat mitzvah much since our sleepover. Something else has been taking up all my brain space lately," Lily says. Then she blurts out, "I think my dad is dating someone."

Everyone stops sewing for a moment. "No way," Sophia says, the unwelcome thought of her own dad dating someone popping into her mind. "How do you know?"

"I don't know anything for certain," Lily says. She keeps her eyes down as she begins to sew the stripes of mint and white fabric together. "But he's been whistling a lot lately. And he was out with a 'friend' three nights this past week. And! A few weeks ago, when we were at dinner, I noticed he had a notification from Bumble!"

"Whoa," Ava says slowly. "That is a *lot* of evidence. How do you feel about him dating?"

"It's hard," Lily muses. "I mean, first of all, I don't even know if he really has a girlfriend. I'm doing some extra snooping to see what I can find. I haven't found much proof outside of what I just mentioned. It's just... I want him to be happy. But I'm not ready for anyone new in our lives yet. I'm finally sort of getting used to it being just the two of us, you know?"

"That makes total sense," Sophia says. Her fingers assemble a checked pattern using patches of metallic silver and gold fabrics, but her mind is far away. "I know having divorced parents doesn't compare, but I would have a really hard accepting either of my parents moving on until we were settled into our new routine."

"Yeah, exactly," Lily says. "I think I just need to tell him I'm not ready for him to date yet."

"I'm sure he'll understand," Maya says. "He's your dad."

"Yeah..." Lily says, trailing off as she stares blankly at her sewing machine.

Sophia catches Maya's eyes as they both look worriedly at Lily. Maya clears her throat. "So, Sophia, what's the plan for tomorrow?"

Sophia lights up, remembering tomorrow night is her turn to host their sleepover. "I have tryouts tomorrow until five o'clock, so how about we meet at six at my house? The only thing is you'll have to remind your parents to pick you up early Saturday morning. My mom is super intense about us beating the traffic into the city, so we'll be leaving around eight."

Her friends start buzzing about what movies they should watch for their sleepover. But Sophia feels a tinge of nervousness as she remembers tomorrow is also her dance audition. *What if I don't make it into the hip-hop program? And I just made such a big deal about it to everyone. This could be so embarrassing...*

Sophia's *heart feels like it just might beat out* of her chest. She is the last to do her routine in tryouts today, which she now believes is the absolute worst time to go. Not only did she have two whole hours to let her already massive nerves build before the performance, but she had to spend those hours watching the routines of the dozens of other wildly talented girls trying out for the program.

*Breathe,* Sophia reminds herself. *If this doesn't work out, you can try out again next year! Most of these girls have been dancing their whole lives. You just got started.*

The music starts playing and Sophia silently counts herself in. All things considered, her routine goes pretty well. She knows she is by no means the best of the girls crammed into the gym right now. But she doesn't think she's the worst either.

Now comes the worst part: the waiting. Her breath catches when she finally sees Coach Alessi stand up with a clipboard in hand.

"Girls, I want to start by thanking you all for coming out here today," she begins. "We saw some real effort. Although we can only admit half of you into the program, we strongly encourage those of you who don't make it to try again next year."

*See?* Sophia says to herself. *There's always next year.*

"Now, I've never been one to beat around the bush, so I'll just dive right in," Coach Alessi says. "The following girls will be joining the prized Charis Academy Dance Program this year: Sophia Ito..."

"Um, sorry, did you just say Sophia Ito?" Sophia blurts out before her brain can process what just happened.

"Yes," Coach Alessi confirms. "That's you, right? Welcome to Charis Dance."

*No way. No way. NO WAY.* Sophia wants to jump out of her seat in the bleachers and squeeze Coach Alessi with a hug, but she knows she must maintain her cool. *Other girls didn't make it. Just sit here calmly until she finishes reading the list and freak out later.*

"I made it!" Sophia squeals as soon as she throws open the door to her mom's car after practice. "I made it! She called my name out first! I was the last to do the routine, which was torture. But then she called my name out *first!*"

"I am so proud of you, honey," her mom says. "See? Hard work always pays off!"

"Wait," Sophia says, noticing a white gift bag on the front seat. "What's this?"

"Open it," her mom says, a smile widening across her face. "I brought you a little something."

Sophia gets in the car and clicks in her seatbelt. Before she manages to tear apart the pink tissue paper inside the bag, she spots a piece of reflective fabric.

"Whoa," Sophia gasps, pulling out the reflective joggers and the black cropped hoodie. "Mom, this is the perfect hip-hop outfit! Where did you get it?"

Her mom gives her a warm smile. "I actually made it. I've been secretly working on it ever since you told me you wanted to try out for the program."

"But I thought you don't really like sewing," Sophia says, remembering the many times she and Baba got rejected trying to convince her mom to sew with them.

"I *don't*," her mom says with a laugh. "But I had some fabric lying around, so I thought I'd give it a shot. Besides, it feels more special this way, right?"

"It really does," Sophia says, inspecting the stitching around the outfit. "And your sewing is so good. This looks like something they would sell at a store!"

"Thanks, hon," her mom says. "Gigi did teach me a thing or two growing up. And I wanted to make sure it was perfect for you."

Sophia stares, still in awe of the outfit. "What would you have done with this if I didn't make the team?"

"Oh, Soph," her mom says. "There was never a doubt in my mind that you would make that team."

"Thanks, Mom," Sophia says. "This really means a lot."

"You're welcome," her mom replies with a grin. "But please, just promise me that you will not wear that outfit anywhere near the country club."

"What?" Sophia asks, confused. "Why not? I told you already, your sewing is good. This looks like a professional put it together."

"It's not that," her mom says. "It's just the whole... style. You know what I mean."

"Um, no, I don't get it," Sophia says, her cheeks burning. "You're the one who made me this. And I thought you were *happy* about me doing hip-hop. It was our thing!"

"And it still is," her mom says as she drives. "You know what I mean about the outfit. Gigi would be *mortified*. She already has a hard enough time seeing you in ripped jeans."

"But why?" Sophia feels her heart sinking. "Why would Gigi be mortified? And why would you even care if she was?"

"It's not just Gigi, sweetie," her mom says. "It's everyone in our circle. Your hip-hop outfit would be cute for New York City and I'm more than happy to let you wear it practicing around the house... but it's just not very Main Line friendly, you know?"

Sophia held back tears. *Why does she care what's "Main Line friendly" anyway?*

When they finally get back home, Sophia quickly goes to her room, puts her new outfit on, and gives her dad a call.

"Dad! Guess what!" Sophia says as soon as his face materializes across her phone screen. "You are going to *freak*."

"Hmm. Well, it's Friday and you're wearing a cool hip-hop outfit," her dad muses from where he's sitting atop the recliner in his living area. "Did you make the program?"

"Yes! And she called my name first!" Sophia squeals. "Ugh, Dad. It was so stressful. There were, like, fifty girls there. And everyone had to go one by one and do their routines for Coach Alessi while she just sat there silently taking notes. Oh, and I had to go *last*."

"Sounds nerve-wracking," her dad says. "When did she say who was in and who wasn't?"

"Well, that was the one nice part of going last," Sophia admits. "She announced the people who made the team pretty shortly after I went. But even those few minutes waiting for her to read the names off her clipboard were torture."

"Okaasan! Guess what!" Sophia's dad calls to Baba, who seems to be cooking in the kitchen. "Sophia made the dance program!"

"That's my girl!" Baba yells. "We will celebrate tomorrow!"

"Yes, Soph, we are expecting a full performance of your

routine tomorrow in the new outfit," her dad says. "Then we'll do a celebratory dinner wherever you want to eat."

"Soph!" her mom yells from downstairs. "Your friends are here!"

"Shoot, Dad, I've got to go," Sophia sighs. "Really wish you were both here. Like, a lot."

"We'll see you tomorrow!" her dad reminds her before hanging up.

Sophia slowly walks down the stairs. She takes a deep breath and tries to recapture her excitement, especially since she's seeing her P4F friends now. But a small part of her feels sad after talking to her dad and Baba. *New York City*, Sophia thinks to herself. *Where I don't have to care if my clothes are "Main Line friendly."*

As she walks outside into the yard where her friends are, Sophia can't help but notice Ava's lacy white dress and the wide-legged jeans Maya paired with a plaid button-down. *Why would Gigi judge me for what I wear?* Sophia thinks. *My friends and I all have different styles, but we respect each other's taste.* Waving to her friends, she admires the spread on the patio table and feels her stomach growl. They were going to be having Shabbat dinner later, but for now, her mom has laid out Spanish tapas-style appetizers to get them started for the evening.

"This is next level," Gracie says, plopping a couple bacon-wrapped dates onto her plate. Today she's wearing patent vegan leather shorts and a mesh turtleneck tank that makes her look super punk rock, especially since she's standing next to Lily, who's in a lavender collared midi dress. "A full Spanish appetizer spread, complete with patatas bravas, bacon wrapped dates, Spanish ham, yummy cheeses, and croquettes? Soph, your mom is the best."

"What are these?" Maya asks, peering close to the plate to read what the label says. She stuffs a bite of chicken into her mouth and sighs. "Okay, potatas bravas might be my new favorite food."

"And we haven't even made our way over to the beverage table yet!" Ava says, gesturing over to the table of fresh-pressed juices set up by their firepit. "This is paradise."

"Whoa, you're all giving my mom a *lot* of credit," Sophia jokes. "But I will say, this is pretty good."

"Wait, how are we even discussing the food when we should be celebrating!" Maya turns to Sophia and claps her hands. "Congratulations, Soph!"

"Yeah!" Ava says. "I heard only half the girls made the cut."

"It was pretty cutthroat," Sophia says. "I can't believe I made it."

"Well, you definitely *look* like a hip-hop dancer," Gracie says, appreciatively taking in the outfit as Sophia jokingly spins around in a circle.

"Agreed," Ava says with a nod. "Did you get that outfit in New York? I haven't seen anything that *spectacular* anywhere around here."

"My mom actually made it for me," Sophia says, her voice coming out a little softer than usual. "And she doesn't even normally like sewing. She surprised me with it once I made the team."

"Really?" Maya asks, her eyes wide with amazement. "Your mom is a great seamstress! It looks professional!"

Lily nods in agreement. "It really does, Soph. It's super New York too. You should wear it this weekend!"

"I probably should, considering my mom made it super clear that it's not an outfit she wants me to be wearing out and about around here," Sophia says with an eye roll.

"What?" Gracie asks. "But didn't she make it for you?"

"Yep," Sophia says. "And she's fine with me wearing it to hip-hop practice or in New York, but she says I can't wear it anywhere near the country club or my Gigi because apparently my new style isn't 'Main Line friendly' enough." She looks down at her plate and suddenly doesn't feel hungry.

"Hey," Ava says, putting down a croquette. "What's the

matter, Soph?"

"I just... I keep thinking about New York City," Sophia blurts out. "Even when awesome things happen here, I feel like my heart is just always there. Obviously I love you guys and I love my life here. But I just feel like, I don't know—maybe I would be happier if I lived there full-time and came back here for the weekends."

All the girls stop eating and stare at Sophia as she fidgets nervously in her seat.

"Whoa," Gracie says. "That's major."

Sophia takes a deep breath. "I know. It's the first time I've said it out loud, but I think it's how I feel. Maybe I need to talk to my dad first, then my mom. I'm not sure if he could even handle having me that often. His schedule is ridiculous, but my baba is always there too, so maybe..." Sophia throws her hands up in frustration. "I don't know. Nothing can happen right now. Maybe not even until high school. But it's just something I'm thinking about."

"That makes sense," Maya says kindly. "But you should let them know now. You know, since they're finalizing the big D."

A throat clears and Sophia's mom suddenly appears from behind her with a filled pitcher in hand. "Hey, girls! Brought you some more watermelon juice."

"Thanks, Mom," Sophia says, jumping up a bit guiltily. *Did she hear anything?* she wonders. She looks at her mom's too-wide smile and looks back down. "Your spread is a big hit."

"Seriously, Ms. Beck," Gracie adds. "This is, like, the most delicious meal ever."

"I'm glad you girls enjoyed," Sophia's mom replies, her voice slightly shaky. "I'll just be inside, so let me know if you need me!" Sophia watches as her mom ducks back into the house and feels her shoulders drop.

"Anyway, enough with the New York talk," Sophia says. "It stresses me out thinking about it. I just wanted you to know where my head has been, you know? You're my best friends."

"Aw, Soph," Ava says, giving her a tight hug. "Whatever happens, we'll be here for you."

"Yep," Gracie agrees. "I mean, your worst-case scenario is being stuck here with us five days a week, so things really aren't so bad."

Sophia cracks a smile. "You're right," she says to Gracie. "It's not like there's nothing going on here."

"Yeah, we had the charity show!" Maya says. "Maybe we should come up with another event like that so we can work toward something."

"Actually, I have a kind of big idea I've been meaning to run by you guys," Gracie says.

"What is it?" Sophia asks.

Gracie has a nervous smile on her face. "Okay, so since our fashion show was such a hit... what if we opened up our own online shop to sell the things we make?"

The girls stare open-mouthed at Gracie.

"That would be *epic*!" Sophia exclaims, her mind already flooding with dozens of ideas for what to sell. "Our own business?! So cool. Even if I did go to New York, I could still contribute on weekends. I have a sewing machine at my dad's!"

"Yeah," Lily says with a nod. "And we could sell things we know people our age would want! Like iPad covers."

"Or stockings when the weather gets colder!" Maya chimes in. "And maybe even clothes?"

Sophia notices Ava is quiet and turns to her. "What do you think, Ava?"

"Love these ideas, but I am already overscheduled," Ava says with a frown. "Can we postpone this convo until after fall break? I feel like I need some time."

"Sure, Aves," Sophia says, feeling for her stressed-out friend. "No worries. Besides, we already have a *lot* going on this semester with Lily's bat mitzvah coming up."

Everyone agrees, nodding, before Gracie adds, "*Clueless* is still the most iconic theme ever."

"Fully agreed! The *most* iconic theme for a party ever," Ava says. "I may be busy, but let me just go on the record and say I have *not* been too busy to start sewing my Dionne outfit."

"I haven't started working on it," Sophia says. "But I was thinking maybe I would be Amber. I can get a red wig and everything."

"That would be amazing!"

"I think I'm a natural Tai," Gracie chimes in. "Pre-makeover, of course. When she was grunge and awesome."

"Okay, I know this may be weird," Maya begins in. "But I thought it could be fun to do a take on Miss Geist?"

"I *love* that!" Lily says excitedly. "So out of the box!"

Lily starts telling the girls about her upcoming bat mitzvah plans while Sophia takes a minute to think about everything she has going for herself here in Lower Merion. She'll be starting hip-hop, she already has P4F, plus she has her social life with her friends. Yet something inside still feels uneasy.

*This is what makes things hard,* she thinks to herself. *No matter which life I choose, I'm leaving another one behind.*

# fourteen

*S*ophia *takes a deep breath and looks down at* her outfit. *Baggy reflective joggers? Check. Cropped black hoodie? Check.* To complete the look, Sophia paired the outfit with a vintage pair of Nike high-tops she found with Baba at a thrift shop in East Village earlier today. *Even if I'm not actually good at hip-hop, I definitely nailed the look of cool hip-hop dancer,* she muses.

"All right, Soph," Sophia's dad says from where he's facing her seated on the chocolate-colored cloud couch in their living area. "Let's see the routine!"

"Yes!" Baba claps her hands excitedly from where she's seated beside him. "I cannot wait to see Sophi-chan shine!"

Alan rolls his eyes. "*Relax,* you guys," he says, from where he's sitting in the corner playing chess against himself. "Soph's really not that great. Trust me. I've been watching her and Mom practice all week. Her forward step is kind of tough to watch."

"Gee, thanks, Alan," Sophia says. "I didn't realize you were such a hip-hop connoisseur."

"Sophia, Sophia, Sophia," he says, shaking his head. "You always underestimate me."

"Kids, simmer down," her dad interjects. "Come on, Soph. I don't care if you're the worst. You were good enough to make the program, right?"

"That's right," she says, beaming at the memory of her name being called out by Coach Alessi. "Okay, I'm ready. Play the music!"

"Industry Baby," by Lil Nas X and Jack Harlow, starts blaring through the speakers and Sophia launches into the routine. She's practiced it so much that at this point, she doesn't even have to think about it anymore. The moves just sort of flow out of her muscles on their own. By the time she's finished, her dad and her baba are out of their seats, giving her a standing ovation. Even Alan has set down his chess pieces for a moment to clap.

"Okay, that wasn't that bad. Maybe the practice is helping," Alan says with a shrug before turning his attention back to his chessboard.

"Or maybe it's just being in New York," Sophia adds, plopping down next to her dad on the couch. "I love being here."

"Not as much as I love having you," her dad says, planting a kiss on top of her head. "Baba and I get so lonely here without you kids running around."

"Well, what if we were around more?" Sophia suggests.

"I would love that," her dad says. "But the only solution would be for you to come straight here after school on Fridays, and I don't want you to miss Shabbat with your friends."

"But what if that wasn't the *only* solution?" Sophia presses, feeling a little more confident. "What if we swapped the schedule around and I spend Monday through Friday here, then went back to the Main Line for the weekends?"

"Are you unhappy there, Sophi-chan?" her baba asks, her eyes growing with concern.

"Everything is fine," Sophia says quickly. "I'm not *unhappy*. I just... it's like this outfit, for example."

"I love it!" her dad says. "Great look."

"I think Bella Hadid would approve," her baba says with a smile. She knows Sophia's ultimate style icon, of course. "Very cool."

"Well, Mom made it, but she says I'm not allowed to wear it to the country club," Sophia says. "Because it's not 'Main Line friendly.' But it's not just the outfit. Sometimes I feel like who I *am* isn't really Main Line friendly."

"You feel more comfortable here in the city?" her dad asks, wrapping his arm around her.

"Yeah," Sophia says with a nod. "I do. I just feel like I belong here. I'm not saying I need to move here now or anything. Just... maybe when I go to high school, I could apply to some schools here? I can ask Lyla where she's thinking of going."

"You don't think you would miss your friends too much?"

her baba asks. "What about Ava?"

"Um, hello," Alan says, waving a hand in the air from where he's been playing chess against himself. "And me. Won't you miss me?"

"Maybe you could come with me, Alan," Sophia suggests. "We could both switch our schedules."

"No thank you," Alan says. "I don't mind spending my weekends here, but I'm a suburb guy myself. This hustle and bustle of the big city is a bit too much for me."

"This is a big decision, Sophia," Baba says. "Make sure you really think it through."

"I would miss my friends a lot," Sophia says slowly. "And I wouldn't be able to make P4F classes if I was here during the weekdays... I guess I have to think about it more. But it's something I'm considering. I mean, if you are up for it."

"I'm willing to do whatever it takes to make sure you're happy, Soph," her dad says. "We can discuss your moving here for high school when you're ready."

"Hopefully you'll come to your senses by then," Alan says. "I know you're the older one here. But let's face it, you would be so lost without me."

Sophia chuckles at her little brother. He really does have a point. All these new changes in her family life have been tough, but at least she's had Alan by her side every step of the way.

"We'll see," Sophia tells him. "I'll keep my options open for now."

Sophia feels her muscles relax a little bit. Knowing that moving to New York could be an option if she really wants it to be one makes her feel a lot more settled.

"Now, who wants to watch a movie?" her baba asks, turning the TV on. "We haven't had a nice movie night in a while."

"A movie night sounds perfect," Sophia says, letting her head rest on her baba's lap. "How about *The Parent Trap*? We haven't watched that in so long."

When her parents first separated, watching *The Parent Trap* became a tradition for Sophia and Alan when they were at their dad's house. Sophia doesn't wish her parents would get back together like the parents in the movie do, but something about seeing other kids with divorced parents makes her feel a little better.

"Yes!" Alan shouts, dropping his chess pieces and making his way over to the couch. "Man, I love this movie."

"I'll order some pizza," Sophia's dad says. "Everyone good with Rubirosa?"

A giant smile breaks across Sophia's face. Rubirosa is her favorite pizza in New York City, maybe even the world.

"I am *more* than good with Rubirosa," Sophia says. "Just make sure to get a tie-dye pie!"

"And a sausage and broccolini one for me, please!" Alan chimes in.

"All right, one tie-dye and one sausage and broccolini coming right up," her dad says, placing the order on his phone. "And maybe a salad, just so we get some veggies in."

The pizzas arrive and the movie begins. As the stepmom Meredith Blake makes her entrance, a horrible thought enters Sophia's mind. *What if Dad falls in love with an evil woman? Even if she's not evil, am I ready for him to fall for anyone?* Her dad did say he was lonely earlier. And if he gets lonely here, would he maybe be dating? Isn't that what adults do when they're lonely?

The thought hits Sophia like a punch in the gut. She loves her dad and she wants him to be happy, but she just doesn't know if she's ready for him to be with anyone else.

"Um, Dad?" Sophia asks. "Can I ask you something?"

"Can it wait until after the movie?" Alan groans. "Sheesh!"

"It's just gonna keep bugging me if I don't say it," Sophia says as her dad pauses the movie. "But, um, are you dating anyone?"

There's a long pause. "I am seeing some friends," her dad admits. "But I'm not dating anyone seriously. I'm not ready for that yet."

"Good," Sophia says, letting out a sigh of relief. "Me neither."

"Me neither," Alan adds softly. "The *last* thing we need is a Meredith Blake taking over this apartment."

"There will be no evil stepmoms here, don't you worry about *that*," their baba reassures them. "Not on my watch."

When the movie ends, Baba says goodnight and heads back to her place, but Sophia and Alan stay in the living room a bit longer watching shows with their dad. Sophia nestles in under his arm, feeling warm and happy. These are the sorts of moments she missed the most, the ones where they are just hanging out. The three of them end us falling asleep right there on the couch watching old reruns of *The Goldbergs*.

The next morning, Sophia wakes up to a call from her mom.

"Hello?" Sophia answers, still groggy.

"Good morning, sleepyhead," her mom says. "I'm about

five minutes away, if you and Alan want to get your stuff together and start heading down."

"Um, okay," Sophia says, a pang of disappointment striking her. "See you soon."

She shakes her brother, who is soundly sleeping on the other side of their dad. "Come on, Alan. Mom is gonna be here in five."

"Okay," Alan says, slowly getting up.

Sophia's dad cracks open his eyes and blinks sleepily at them. "I'm going to miss you two."

"Next week do you want to do chess in Battery Park again?" Alan asks. "That was fun."

"Count me in," her dad says, giving Alan a kiss on the cheek.

"Bye, Dad," Sophia says, her eyes welling up with tears. "Ugh, I don't know why I'm crying. It's just... the more we do this, the harder it gets to leave."

"Oh sweetie," her dad says, pulling her in for a hug. "But like I said last night, we can discuss the high school thing when you're ready. This setup might not have to be permanent."

"I know," Sophia says, wiping the tears away. "I know."

When Alan and Sophia finally make their way into their mom's car, Sophia notices her mom is acting a bit weird. She can't quite put her finger on what exactly is off, but something just doesn't feel quite normal.

"Did you guys have fun with your dad?" her mom asks.

"It was awesome," Alan says with a yawn. "I got to play chess all day and Sophia got these new shoes to go with her hip-hop outfit. She did her dance for Baba and Dad and, honestly, she wasn't bad. Then Dad got us Rubirosa and he let us fall asleep on the couch with him watching TV! You *never* let us fall asleep on the couch watching TV."

"Well, countless studies show that screen time before bed disrupts your sleep," her mom notes, her voice still obviously strained. "But I'm glad you had fun."

Five minutes later, they notice Alan is already snoring in the backseat.

"I can't believe he fell asleep so quickly," Sophia quietly says to her mom. "I guess you were right about the screen thing."

"Mm-hmm," her mom says with a nod.

The two of them sit there for a few seconds in total silence, save for Alan's occasional snores from the backseat.

"We watched *The Parent Trap*," Sophia says, trying to break the silence. "Don't you love that movie?"

"Yes," her mom says through what Sophia knows is her fake smile. "Love it."

They drive for a few more minutes in complete silence until Sophia can't take it anymore.

"Is everything okay, Mom?" she asks. "You're acting kind of weird."

"...Okay, fine," her mom says with a sigh, her eyes still fixated on the road ahead. "I overheard you talking to your friends on Friday, Sophia. About moving to New York. And... I want you to be happy. But, you know, I would be lying if I said it didn't break my heart a bit."

"Mom, it's just an idea," Sophia says, trying not to look at her mom's sad face. "I just feel more at home in New York. It's not a you-versus-Dad thing, okay?"

"I know," her mom says, taking one hand off the steering wheel to wipe the tears streaming down her face. "You're right. I need to be the adult here and not take it so personally." She pauses for a second before adding, "Is this move something you're absolutely set on?"

"Not really," Sophia says. "It's just something I've been thinking about. And even if I did do it, I wouldn't want to make the move until high school anyway."

"Okay, then how about we just discuss it in the future?" her mom suggests. "When you're ready to start looking at high schools, we can tour some in New York and in our area."

"That sounds great," Sophia says. "Thanks, Mom."

Sophia looks out the window as they inch closer to the Holland Tunnel in the bumper-to-bumper traffic. Her chest feels less heavy now that she talked to her mom, but her head is still confused. *Is living here full-time what I really want?* She feels grateful it's not a decision she has to worry about right now.

Sophia didn't know how fun school at Charis could be until joining the dance program. Ever since hip-hop practice on Tuesday, Sophia feels like she's at a whole new school. On her first day she made a few new friends from the dance program who she really likes, and now she's eating lunch with them. Ava even left her own table to sit with them once! Plus, Sophia has been getting through her homework faster than ever so that she can get back to practicing the routine Coach Alessi taught them.

Before she knows it, Friday evening arrives and the girls are at Maya's house. Since this week is Maya's turn to host the sleepover, the girls meet in the Alvarezes' kitchen for a hybrid of their family's Pizza Friday tradition and the P4F girls' version of Shabbat dinner. Maya's family has been doing monthly Pizza Fridays for years, with all their friends and family gathered to munch on delicious pizzas Maya and her family cook using fresh produce from the farmer's market. Rather than immediately joining everyone else outside, the girls would enjoy their pizzas inside in the kitchen with their version of a Shabbat.

Sophia watches from across the table as Mrs. Alvarez lights the second candle. "I'll leave you girls to continue your Shabbat without me," she says with a warm smile before heading back outside to her guests. Once she leaves, Sophia instinctively brings her hands to her eyes. All five girls do the same motion three times, then cover their eyes as Lily does the Jewish blessing. Once Lily is finished, Gracie reads "A Friend," by Gillian Jones, the poem they had picked out that first Shabbat dinner: At this point, Gracie knows the poem by heart.

When she's done with her recital, the girls all dig into their pizzas. As Sophia grabs a juice for herself, she excitedly tells them about the new moves she learned today in hip-hop.

"Soph, you gotta show us how to moonwalk later," Gracie says as she takes a bite of the truffle honey pie in front of her.

"Speaking of which, how is dance class going?" Lily asks as she helps herself to a slice of the squash pizza.

"It's definitely a lot to handle with homework and P4F class," Sophia admits, thinking about the late nights she had to get all of her homework done. "But I don't care because I love it. I mean, I love fashion and it will *always* be my first love. But it's kind of nice having another hobby, you know? Plus, I really like my coach and the girls in the dance program."

"Have thought more about moving to New York?" Maya asks, her eyes giving away her concern.

"I already gave Ava a little refresher at school this week," Sophia says, helping herself to a slice of the Brussels sprout bacon pie. "But basically, I talked about it with my dad when I was in New York. We decided that if I'm still considering it when the time comes to apply for high schools, we can discuss it then."

"That seems fair," Gracie says with a nod. "Did you talk to your mom too?"

"I was *hoping* to hold off on that conversation for a bit longer," Sophia admits. "But she actually overheard us when we were in my backyard last week."

"Oh no!" Lily's eyes grow wide. "Is everything okay?"

"I think so," Sophia says. "She said we could discuss the move when I'm ready to."

"Were her feelings hurt?" Maya asks. "I know you were worried about that."

"Um, yeah, I think at first she felt really bad," Sophia says, frowning at the awkward memory. "But it's nothing personal about her. I just really love New York City. And I think she got it."

"Phew!" Ava reaches over to give Sophia a side hug. "Now you can just enjoy the rest of seventh grade and deal with this big decision when the time comes to deal with it."

"Yep," Sophia agrees, relief washing over her body. "But anyway. Enough about me. Aves, are you still swamped? I feel like I barely even saw you this week at school."

"Swamped is an understatement," Ava sighs. "I had *so*

much going on. Next week horseback riding is over, which is a bummer, but at least soon I'll have some more free time on my hands."

"Really?" Gracie has a hopeful look on her face and darts a glance at Maya, who nods.

"In that case, and feel free to shut this down," Maya begins, "but do you think it's enough free time for us to actually start working on Gracie's idea?"

Sophia's face lights up as she remembers the online store Gracie had mentioned the week prior at her house. *Are we really going to sell our own designs? That would be amazing!*

Ava taps her chin thoughtfully. "Without horseback riding, I think that should give me more time, plus the idea sounds like so much fun. I still might have to wait until after fall break to really give it my all, but I think we could start mapping out our idea."

"Yay!" Sophia loudly cheers, before clapping a hand over her mouth. "Sorry. That was way too loud. This is just so exciting!" she says in a quieter voice.

"You're telling *me*," Gracie says, smiling ear to ear. "I've been thinking about it for months now!"

"Wow, I cannot believe we are going to be businesswomen," Lily says.

"So, what are we thinking exactly?" Maya asks. "An Etsy shop?"

"That was my original idea," Gracie says. "But the more I think about it, Etsy seems complicated with having to schedule shipments and stuff like that."

"But where would we sell our products then?" Ava asks. "It's not like we have a store we can just rent out."

"Well, that's not really true," Gracie notes. "I haven't talked it through with her yet, but I was thinking I could ask my mama if we could start the business off by selling some of our creations at Zoey's Closet. I mean, that's where we make most of our stuff anyway, right? Why not just sell it straight from the source?"

"Gracie, I *love* that idea!" Sophia says. "Plus, the street Zoey's Closet on is always filled with people. I bet all we would have to do is display our stuff in the windows and customers would just come in and buy them."

"I think we should still make an Instagram and maybe even a TikTok," Ava says, getting more into it now. "Just to promote the store and show people the designs they can find there. I can handle that. My parents always say they could see me doing well in social media marketing."

"Great idea! I kind of want to get started right away. Maya, do you think your mom and dad will care if we just stay in your room today?" Sophia asks. "What do you girls think of brainstorming some items for our new business?"

"I have some paper and colored pencils upstairs," Maya says. "We can sketch some designs that we can sew as soon as we get back to Zoey's Closet."

"This is so exciting!" Lily says excitedly, her voice a little louder than usual. "I think I'll design a beanie I can finger knit. Finger knitting is my strong suit, so I might as well start there."

Sophia's mind is brimming with a million ideas before she settles on one. "I want to sew up a loosely fitted pair of joggers," she says. "I can make it upcycling whatever light fabric I can find laying around my house later. But I have a really cool vision."

The girls clear the table of their pizzas and Maya hands out paper and pencils to everyone. As Sophia helps Ava design a coat with two types of fabric, Sophia realizes that tomorrow at this time, she'll be in New York again. But at least right now, she's not rushing to go anywhere.

# about the author

**Tina Wells** is the author of twelve books, including the bestselling tween fiction series *Mackenzie Blue*, and its spinoff series, *The Zee Files*. She is also a business strategist, advisor, and the founder of RLVNT Media, a multimedia content venture serving entrepreneurs, tweens, and culturists with authentic representation. She has been featured on TV and in multiple publications, including *O, The Oprah Magazine, Marie Claire, Forbes, USA Today,* NPR, and the *New York Times*. *Sofia's Struggle* is the second book in the Stitch Clique book series. Tina lives on the East Coast but likes to travel and share her passion to encourage and uplift young people.